Manual Labor

Manual Labor

a novel by **Labor**

FREDERICK BUSCH

A New Directions Book

Manufactured in the United States of America
First published clothbound and as New Directions Paperbook 376 in 1974
Published simultaneously in Canada by McClelland & Stewart, Ltd.

Library of Congress Cataloging in Publication Data

Busch, Frederick, 1941–
    Manual labor.

    (A New Directions Book)
    I. Title.
PZ4.B9767Man   [PS3552.U814]   813'.5'4   74–6286
ISBN 0–8112–0535–5
ISBN 0–8112–0536–3 (pbk.)

New Directions Books are published for James Laughlin
by New Directions Publishing Corporation,
333 Sixth Avenue, New York 10014

For Ben

Manual Labor

*A*FTER *I DIED they moved from Massachusetts and they bought a house and acres of land in New Hampshire where they rose early and worked all day at projects with their hands.*

"You forget with your hands" *my tall blond father said.*

My mother, who was dark and snaky, told him "Sometimes you forget things for a while when you do nearly anything at all. Aren't you the one they elected president of all the romantics over six feet tall?"

My father—he was peeling logs for a fence along the road—stopped working but stayed where he was, flat along the log he straddled, legs planted wide, sweat everywhere on him. He smiled as if she had forgiven him transgressions and he quietly said "Yes."

Now when they lost me she kept sliding on her own bloody footprints (my slimed tissue) up and down the linoleum hallway, bedroom to bathroom and back, and back, the foot-shapes of blood becoming thicker, more like a crimson slush,

1

until she whinnied and went white and went down. While she was unconscious the rest of me came out. And he found us in our blood and saved her life. I am their bled-away fetus, the baby whom they lost in the middle of month nine after nine years of marriage. I am the baby talking that was lost before they sold and bought (and constantly loved in their frantic bed when they were sick of one another's flesh, even); so that they came there after nine years and seven months of childless marriage with a new fetus in her flat belly, and some money for a house, and the need to repair things with their hands. I am a baby who died, the voice of romance, and these are some of the dreams I have witnessed in the actual world.

*M*y *father in the cold stone cellar with a pile of lally columns on the floor behind him, like gray enameled faggots. Hunched from his height, and shivering as his sweat evaporated off, he searched the beams with his flashlight, brushed cobwebs from his face—spitting as he did, as if the spiders were trying to enter his mouth—and ran the light along the dark brown foot-wide hand-adzed beams, chipped and split and mossy with webs, clusters of spider eggs, the empty shells of insects trapped and eaten. Upstairs my mother walked from sill to sill along the beam that was sagging, canting their house so that doorways were crooked and doors would not close, so that an egg might roll from one side of the kitchen to the other and crush itself against the wall. As she followed the beam she called "Here!" and banged the fir floorboards with a broomstick. Downstairs his light jumped to follow her complaint. Together they traced by cry and response the crookedness they had to fix.*

When they had gone the length of their leaning house he called "Okay."

She banged the floorboards and shouted "Here!"

He said "Okay, I have it."

2

She banged the floorboards and shouted "Here!"

"Yes—okay, love. I have it."

"Here!"

"I said I *have* it!"

"Here!"

He howled "I said I have the fucking beam!"

Her footsteps shuffled, stopped, circled softly and moved on. He squatted on the stone cellar floor and held his face.

Then, soon, still crouching, his flashlight picking up corroded pipe, the giant heat-tubes of the coal furnace converted for oil and wrapped in asbestos, heaps of mildewed cardboard and bundles of newspaper stacked like hay, he went back to the screw jacks and made arrangements to straighten things out. Four flat jack-bases went on the floor beneath the beam, about eight feet apart and in a row. Then, clamping the light in his armpit—showing sudden useless views of fieldstone wall or the bottom of the floor—he inserted a column in each base and adjusted the turnscrews until the columns pressed up at the sagging beam. Near the top of each column a steel pin stuck out, and he turned each one, and every column in its turn screwed up against the beam and held there, artificial palms pressing. The light went around and stayed on the stacked corroding pipe; he hunted through nipples and elbows and nuts until he found a small round length that he carried to the first lally column he'd put up, the first place she had struck at, shouting. He fitted the pipe around the pin, wiping slime and web off on his tee-shirt front, and turned. He smiled his teeth and turned again, while the flashlight lay dark on the floor. The house groaned, and he did too.

In darkness, his shoulders pulled in, head bowed, he carried the pipe to the next lally column and turned, and the old wood rumbled as he lifted up the floor. Then he went, blind, to the next one and turned. He turned more. He turned again. And at the final post he pivoted beneath his house and leaned against the column and ached the floorbeam up, and up another turn in darkness, and one more, and her footsteps thumped upstairs

3

and he stopped. He squatted and then on one knee kneeled. The cellar door opened and light fell in. He whispered "What?" He said "What?"

"She said "You pushed too hard.""

"I'm not pushing, I'm turning."

"Turned too hard. We lost a wall."

"We lost a wall."

"You must have pushed the beam up too much. Turned it. The living room has this crack in it now that it didn't used to have. A long diagonal crack."

"Thank you."

"Well we can fix it, can't we?"

"Sure."

"We can plaster it."

"That's right."

"I'm sorry, baby."

"Well."

"As long as we can fix it, though."

My father said "As long.""

M*y mother driving home from the hardware store in their 1965 Ford Ranchwagon 352—gray paint flaked off across the wide hood, a series of wounds revealing the silver primer paint, the last tender skin. She turned left from the two-lane macadam road onto their dirt driveway which was at the end of a short weedy lawn downhill from the house. When she stopped the car in front of the little barn they called garage she turned the motor off and sat before the barn filled with lumber and garden tools and suitcases, piles of old magazines. My father came down from the house in moccasins and shorts, his high wideness glassy with sweat on the fat and muscle someone carries who is thirty-five, who played a college basketball which stressed the set shot and the singularity of*

*men six-four, now small on those same courts. He walked on
his toes and swung his arms and carried his head back, so that
he seemed to look up at the bill of the baseball cap he wore
down on his eyes. He brushed at bugs and held to the top of
the car, leaned down at the off-side window and talked across
the long front seat to her:* "You get the eightpenny nails,
babe?"

*She looked ahead and nodded. Her right hand was over
her left on the wheel, and the bones of her knuckles worked.
The hands were long and thin and tanned, with short cracked
nails, the nails of a workingman. She looked at the moving
bones in her hands and nodded, looked at my father and
looked, then looked out front again and stayed that way.*

*He raised his rump and shifted his wide thighs, planted
his feet, arranged his hands on the roof at the edge of the
door. He looked as if he planned to push the Ford until it
lay on its side, where she sat. He said* "Is it bad news in the
womb? Are you bleeding?"

She said "No. I'm sorry—don't worry, I'm all right. I'm
just deciding to have a tantrum."

"But your body's okay?"

"I can't make a cunning joke about that now."

"What kind of a tantrum?"

She said—her voice went higher, she blushed—"A kind
of sadness tantrum. You know?"

He said, as if he begged her forgiveness, "I *don't* know.
A general all the sadness in the world thing? Your *own* sadness thing? No. What?"

She nodded very quickly. She said "On the hill past all
those phony ski chateaux made of plastic? You know where I
mean?" *He nodded quickly too.* "I was going into town, up the
hill, and this little girl goes past me in the other lane. She was
going down. Maybe she was seven, eight, something like that.
On a bicycle, going down with her legs stuck out, half scared,
half crazy with fun, dungarees and tee-shirt, *all* of that, pig-
tails even. Flying down that hill. And I stopped and watched

5

her come and pass me and go on, rolling crazy, half in control, giggling, and when she was past me I watched her go on down. I could see the road behind me and the road ahead of her, clean and empty, smooth, it was so *beautiful*. Do you understand this?" *He nodded again, slowly this time.* "I mean, I didn't care where she was going. I didn't care whether *she* cared where she was going. If she was going anyplace at all. I just was happy she was on her way. Or no way at all. Had motion that sweet is what I mean"

He said "You're so incredible."

She said "No! Don't tell me anything about this. All right? Don't take this from me."

"Yes."

"And don't be angry."

"No. I won't."

"It's just a tantrum."

"All right. Yours."

"So I kept driving. Can I tell you the rest?"

He nodded once.

"So I kept driving, see, and I'm completely happy. Passive—I was *rest*ing while I drove, I was so damned glad. And I got to the top of the hill, where those chateaux are, and that horrible Virgin-Mary-grotto-blue trailer with the green striped awning in front? There's this little girl, blue polo shirt, blue shorts—little round skinny white legs—and she's standing in the road, looking down the hill where the other one went. Sisters? I don't know. But she was standing there on her little legs, crying. Just crying. Looking down the hill. All she *was* was crying. The big one was supposed to stay with her and she left her alone and took off on her bike, she flew away. All the littler one did was look down the hill with her hands at her sides, crying." *She put her forehead on her hands on the wheel. She said* "I'm sorry, but I have to have a tantrum for that."

He said "Hey. Sweetie—"

She said "No. Why do we have to have kids?"

He pulled his head from the window and looked past the barn and over fields of mustard and devil's-paintbrush to the hillocks that rolled like seas at the base of their mountain. Around it and coming down to them the sky was transparent, as wide as if they stood on a plain. He put his hands in his pockets and looked at the house.

She said "I got the nails."

"Thank you."

"And I wrote a check for paint, all right? I got fifteen gallons of outside semigloss. I want to paint the house."

"What color? Mary-grotto blue?"

"Shit brown."

*M*y *mother watching my father tighten a clamp around a plastic runoff hose behind the house. He didn't have a sprocket wrench to fit the nut, so with cheap chromium-plated pliers—too big for what he worked with—he was turning his wrist and clacking his tool as it slipped off the nut as if he were holding a metal-plated crab by the tail. He was on his back and his legs were spread as he dug his heels in and uselessly turned. He did not talk or stop. My mother in loose low ochre corduroys and a loose men's undershirt was silent—hands tucked into the waistband of her pants, belly slouched forward, breasts barely visible, nipples wide and dark against the shirt—and she stood with her back to the sloping meadow behind the house, she watched only him. Above the bluish grass of the meadow and the ocean green of the hills there was their mountain: always in weather, blurred and purple, mist running down it in the wind as water foams from coastal rocks. She looked at him.*

He worked. He had sliced his thumb against the punched-out clamp's sharp edge and the clamp was loose enough to slide, still, so he jammed the pliers again at the nut that held

7

the clamp that fixed the clear plastic pipe to the metal pipe that protruded through the wall from their bathtub. Like a child about to steal she sidled closer, then went down to her knees between his legs. He held the pliers still. Her eyes looked at nothing. She lay upon him, reached for his wrist; his left hand took the pliers from his right as she closed her eyes and put the cut right thumb to her lips and licked it, squeezed it slowly into her mouth. The pliers remained in his hand.

M y father working to caulk the hole around the bathroom runoff pipe while rain and the sunset came together over their mountain behind them. From the bathroom window my mother said "Supper's ready. All I did was open cans."

"That way you could spend your time on important things."

"I'll get to work tomorrow."

"We have to creosote the fence."

"Okay."

"We haven't *painted* yet."

"Okay!"

"And none of the inside wall work—"

"Yes! Yes: all right, I will do my duty. All right?"

"Hey hon—"

"Never mind."

"Hey hon—"

"Look—"

"Hon: it isn't duty. It's for us."

"For us."

"I didn't know we were a mockery to us."

She said "Okay. Except for one thing. It took you most of the day to arrange for our body water to flow away in a straight line."

"So?"

8

"Nothing. Except we have no idea what we're doing. Except it's August and we won't be ready for winter. One whole day on body water. What I mean is what about the big stuff?"

"All of it's big stuff. Everything is big stuff. Nothing here is *small*."

Like that: in the rain that washed away the caulking he'd applied, he on his knees like a wet bear, she in her window like a princess. She hung her head out and watched the caulking melt. She said "What about when something goes bad?"

He looked at the caulking too and said "You should know."

"What?"

"Nothing could be bad again. What could really be bad?"

"You think we had all that already?"

He said "Most of it. Enough." *She looked at him and nodded and looked, looked, then drew her head back and pulled the screen window closed. He said* "You know? Hon?"

He stayed that way in the rain.

My mother painting the front clapboard brown, my father brushing creosote onto the fence along the road a dozen feet from the house. The sun made the grass look yellow, and they sneezed in the fumes its heat cooked up from their work. They wore the same clothing. They said the same words.

At their cleansing in the mill race far below their house, down a forested hill at the edge of their land. The river was squeezed by high glinty rocks and it poured, exploded onto flat slimed rocks below, then went down onto other flat rocks and narrow foaming deeper places where the banks were high stone walls the mill had stood on. Rusted iron cogwheels, giant bolts,

9

*were in the walls; they bathed in a ruins. The water's collision
was thunder. The air was wet. Everything—the stone, the
cress and teasel, flowers that bobbed in the force of the
sound, their nakedness—was cold. He shouted and cupped his
scrotum, slid from the waterfall down on the slimy flat rocks
to the pool where she stood, hands at her hair, her dark thin
body stretched and beginning to bulge. Her lips were purple
as the veins that showed on her breasts and neck and abdomen.
She jumped when he dropped his hands to her hips from
behind.* He shouted "Go get dressed. You'll get sick."

*She nodded her head, then shook it, let go of her black
long hair and with her hands she made a gesture of disgust.*

He shouted "You have to take care of yourself."

"I can't hear you."

"You have to take *care* of yourself."

"Why?"

"What?"

"I said why?"

"You are a mother" he yelled.

She screamed "Oh no I'm not! Not yet! No!"

"Hey—"

"What?"

"You *want* to be a mother."

"Last time we did this—"

"I can't hear you!"

"Last time I was a mother I died."

"No! No!"

"I don't want to die any more."

"Please—"

"Louder?"

"I don't know what to say."

"What? I *know* you want a baby."

"So do you!"

"Really?"

"Don't you? Don't you?"

"What?"

10

"I don't know what to say."
"What?"

M y father laying a floor downstairs while upstairs my mother plastered walls. The living room was dark, the freshly plastered walls were bright. The crack he had cut in the old dry plaster by lifting the house too hard was covered up.

He set a row of maple boards on black tacky building paper up to the chalkline that showed where the toe molding went. He filled his mouth with nails. Then, crawling backward down the line of boards, he laid a nail in every four inches of wood. He slanted nails six inches apart through the tongue of each board to hold it when he set the next board's groove along the tongue. He cut with a saber saw and nailed and then crawled up the length of the row to start again.

My mother came downstairs, a trowel in her hand, plaster freckled on her arms and face, and she stood behind him as he banged his floor into place. She said "Hey."

He stopped moving. He spread his fingers on the floor and said "Are you all right?"

She said "Don't worry." Then she said "You do good work."

"You should know."
"I do."

He rang his hammer on nails and said "They let you adopt a kid at our age."

"Is that what you'd like us to do? Buy some kid someplace? Secondhand?"

He hit another nail, then shook his head. He said "I want to force—this fucking—"

"World."
"Everything. All of it."
"Yes."

"I want to *force* it to give us our kid that we made."

"Yes. See, I *know* that."

"But?"

"But so let's say it doesn't kill me this time—"

"Us."

"Kill us?"

"I don't want to talk that way."

"Let's say it doesn't, though."

"Let's."

"So?" *she said.*

"What do you mean, *so.* What kind of question is that?"

"After ten years alone together, how do you think we can live with a kid? That's what I mean, *so.* What do we *do?*"

He set his hammer down and spread his fingers flat along the floor. He shook his head.

She said "You see? Maybe we should pray for some disaster soon. I don't know."

She watched him kneel, and then she watched him weep.

*M*y *father repairing the roof. He lay on the black asphalt shingle head down, his torso in a blue workshirt lower than his legs which climbed the pitch above him. He was clearing a path for the aluminum drip cap underneath rake boards with a hack saw, grunting, dripping perspiration in a stream that grew thicker and faster. Beneath him, painting clapboard brown, my mother stopped to watch him sweat. She stepped back away from the house and rubbed her belly with a bony hand. He was golden and haloed in greens at that low angle of sun as he baked upside down.*

My mother said "You look like you're melting."

"I am."

"You're dripping like an icicle."

"Fat wax candle."

12

"Sheep-tallow candle, maybe."

He chuffed and shifted his legs. "Or one of those what-chamacallits, yak-dung butter lamps."

She said "Terrific."

"Yeah, well that adds the element of stink, which is becoming a factor here in case you noticed?"

"Yes," *she said,* "I *thought* there was something someplace rotting."

"Me."

She walked back under the eaves to her painting. She did a strip of clapboard—neatly, precisely, economically, without affection for the wood or paint or process—and she walked back out past the cornices, then down to the end of the roof where he worked. Her brush dripped rich chocolate blots where she walked. She looked at him, dripping upside down and golden above her. She said "Something else is rotting where we left it last year. Remember last year's crop?"

*M*y *mother relaxing on their narrow back porch, my father mowing grass, the sunset drinks prepared. She wore her tight white bell-bottom slacks and a tight white undershirt vest. She leaned against the unpainted doorframe and watched him finish a circle of mowing with his Bolens self-propelled four horsepower machine. He worked always in a circle swinging left so that the chopped grass shooting from the right-side ejector wouldn't fall beneath the blade and give the motor extra work. He was circling on the final patch, she watched him, sat beside the frosted drinks and waited, and he let the mower go and walked before it to brush at the grass where a small pale toad sat paralyzed and then took off. It was a self-propelled machine and he had let his hold go, but not the sprocketed will of its obedient gears. It came the way he had set it to come. She watched it mow his right thumb.*

The machine only paused for his hand, bucked a little,

13

then went on down the incline of high thick blue-green grass, cutting, on down to the base of the meadow, ringing on wood or stones, set in motion, going on.

He bellowed and swung his right hand in a high frantic arc, swung it down, swung it up and down and seized it, squeezed it between his legs as a stung child might. The blood blew up on his face and chest and soaked his groin and thighs to the knees. He screamed "My hand! My hand! What happened to my hand? My hand! My *hand!"*

Her face had no expression when she pushed at her stomach as if she had cramps. She had no expression when she ran to him and never looked at his drained gray face. She pulled the knot of fist from between his legs and squeezed the squeezing hand, then pulled him by his geysering wound to the car. She said "Okay. Okay. Now you're fine. You're okay, that's a love. Okay." *She didn't look at his face. She clutched her own front.*

She didn't look in the rearview mirror to find his face while she drove—with one hand; the other was fisted in her groin—while he lay pulsing in the back of the wagon like a cargo and the roadside firs were poured full of red by the sun that sat on their horizon, beating. And she didn't look when she skidded on the veterinary hospital's gravel drive and sat outside of the low white cinderblock building, pushing at the horn—the one insistent tone of her distress, over and again, again—until a fat young man in coveralls came out and then went in and then came out and started to work on my father's hand which had no thumb and could not wield pliers or hold onto hammers or reach from the length of his outstretched arm to grasp.

*M*y *mother at the bled-out hours of dawn—my father sedated, away in the Nashua hospital they had hauled him to—*

sitting on their white porcelain toilet like a small skinny girl. Her vest was red from blood, her slacks were red and crushed around her ankles on the floor. She squeezed her thin white legs together and held her arms against her chest, her hands against her shivery chin. Her eyes were closed, her body shook, her face was wet with her weeping. She made the sounds of someone very cold. My brother spun in the water below her and sank. She sat that way.

*O*ur *mother at the kitchen window in another night. The moon was misted and their mountain glowed like ice. In her long white nightgown she sat straight up in her chair, her arms against her chest, hands against her chin. Her face was wet. She watched our father, dizzy and bandaged, crawling in little circles, tearing at the grass that had grown high again to find his orphaned thumb.*

A nd *our mother at the window of their extra room upstairs, chilled from a winter of not being heated, the brass bed cold, its damp quilt cold, a feeling of ice on the stained shiny floorboards, a February light that came through the window and glowed on her shiny thin face like the moon on cold stones. It was day, and she had spent the night here, reading two books half through. Neither was open now; the pages of one were wrinkled from hands. She sat at the school child's desk before the window and looked to the light washed with yellows, looked down the road before their house, or across it to the hillside pasture that climbed away under snow. Her fingers were black with ink, and ink was on the wood of the desk, on her lips where she had rubbed, writing, looking away, around, down,*

15

away, and at the pages—puckered from sweat, shuffled, crimped—and she talked on them, the pen's black talon talked for her, scratching in dragged whispers on the white sheets whiter than the snow surrounding them which glinted in the sun or lay around them in shadows as blue as bruises, as black as the ink on her white nightgown's sleeves, and as black as the ink on her mouth: Because you always wanted babies, Mamma. I don't mean you always wanted *your* babies. Though you did. And you had them. You had them. Us. But ours, you wanted ours. And now you're not getting them. I mean, Cassie did have kids. Didn't she, though. Except one was by a man who didn't marry her, so that didn't qualify. And the other ended up broken into pieces in a car, along with Cassie and the other guy who probably wouldn't have married her either, I heard tell (we say it like that in New Hampshire). So that one didn't come across. And then me. *Then us* Oh I know you don't blame me. Only it's the not blaming I can't handle so well right now. As you would know if I would mail this. Do you bet I don't? You bet your life. You bet your ass. You bet your husband. You bet my daddy. You bet. You bet. It's the news you keep on sending me, Mamma. All that news. Flash! Your seventh cousin just dropped four calves fathered by the oxlike paper-products salesman she married in her seventh month. Here are their pictures in the paper. Here is the story written by a semiliterate newspaper columnist. Here are their names, here are their dates. Here is my love and hoping this finds you well, maybe we can drive up in the spring and see how you kids are getting on. Well I am thirty-six, kid, Kidless thirty-six. Dear Mamma: Thank you for the news. I was happy to hear that Cousin Bovina had four kids. You were kind to tell me. I will file the clipping down my husband's throat. When I keep him from sleeping for a couple of nights I will write and tell you nothing, nothing. Not about how his face has no expression any more. And not about how I mainline aspirin. I'm immune! I can pop them all day—buffered, unbuffered, reinforced for cold remedy, in capsules, pills, powders. I can swallow them, shoot them in my arm, stuff them up my ass. Nothing. Nothing takes my headaches away. If I went to a doctor he'd take all my clothes off and fill me full of sperm, I'd blow a half-made baby out my navel in the middle of month nine. Sometimes I dream about infants that cry. Sometimes I wake up. And thank you, Mamma, for the news about Daddy. I'm sorry he works so hard and never comes home. I never come home too. I'm sorry he makes you lonely. Your letters make me lonely too. Sometimes I cry when I read them. Sometimes infants dream they hear me crying. They don't wake up. *We don't sleep* You must be frightened of his heart. I hope it doesn't burst or crack. I haven't talked to him for thirty years. I do not think that I will talk to him. I miss him more than you. At the hospital they made me sign a paper saying my baby was dead. I guess they weren't sure. They should have been. The second time they didn't make me sign because I went later on, when the only proof of death was me. They told me I was proof enough. The doctors were kind. There was a student nurse whose eyes were smeared with crying. The lights in the emergency room looked like now, outside. It's nearly spring. Cold, but nearly spring. Soon we'll have to go outside and do something about springtime. What shall we do? Have projects: finish the roof, and paint the barn, put shingles on the clapboard or paint it a different color, buy a new car, get a job, go running in a meadow, cut the brush behind the house with a scythe. It's nearly spring. It's nearly spring. Did I tell you the one about my husband and me and the halfway fellatio? Seems there was this long lady and her husband in bed of an autumn night or winter. Stop me if you heard this one. And he put his heavy arm under my back and rolled us over so that I was on top. Our tongues together. And he pushed me down with his heavy arms. Down. I knew what it was and so what. I didn't want to but I didn't care. And his little prick was so enormous! I said "Prick. Prick." because he likes to hear that, and I held my lips against it and pushed. I opened my mouth and it sprang inside like a dog

17

coming home from the cold. I didn't want to but I didn't
care. I heard him sigh, I heard his whispering. I said "Mmm"
because he likes that. He was coming, almost, by the time I
had him in.

He said "You know why I like that—forcing you this
way?"

His heavy arms. I stopped. I leaned my head up and it
glistened away from my lips in the dark.

He said "Because you like it. Being forced. Don't you?"

I felt him waiting, his body was down but rising to meet
me. He wanted so much. I couldn't. I couldn't any more. I
said "What?"

"Because you like it so much."

I said "No."

And it is three days later, Mamma, early in the morning
again. Mourning again. Borning again. Boring again. Again.
Three days later and there's snow all over the ground. We have
icicles on the eaves and nothing has changed. Sometimes we
have breakfast and he goes to work. Sometimes he has breakfast and he goes to work. Sometimes I have breakfast. Sometimes I don't. I don't know if I'm tantalizing him or boring him
to death. It used to excite me afterward. First it made me
sick, then it stirred me. One of us would start, and that
wouldn't matter—which one. One of us would start. The other
would pitch right in. Domestic cooperation, he would call it.
Sharing the shit, I'd say. That would be afterward. One of us
would start and the other would help and we would roar and
roar and scream and pound on things and then he would fall
into it. He would fall in, the way a man falls down a hole.
Like turds down a toilet pipe. Or children swimming down,
same thing. And he would pick things up and break them. I'd
cry until my eyes burned. I'd vomit sometimes. Gag. Heave
around the house. We'd nearly always screw later on. We'd
have to. How could we say what couldn't be said? He said it
all with the breaking. Do you remember the set of Victorian
chairs you gave us from your garage? Three out of four we

18

used for kindling. He broke them, two in one night, one on an afternoon that lasted for a year and a half. I wish he would do that now. Or tell me something. Or maybe he has. I've lost some time. I can't remember how we spent the last few months. But I wish I could be easier for him. Or *here*. Here. Wherever this is. The other day—some time back, some time, some time ago—I said "This thing about whiteness that Melville says in *Moby-Dick?*" He looked at me, all blond whiskers and wrinkles and his big lovely mouth. He looked at me and I was very ashamed. I said "I don't mean to be all literary." He looked at me. I said "It's very self-conscious isn't it?" He looked at me and shook his head. He gave me that. He shook his head to say No. I looked at the toast or waffles or whatever he'd made me for breakfast. I said "Thank you." But he walked away, he went to work. I haven't said that any more. You should never thank him. Will you remember that? Do you remember the time we visited you and Daddy's car spun into the mud along your drive and he pushed it out? He's nothing but muscles when he works. Except on me. He used to be soft when he was hard with me. You thanked him and he asked you for a beer. You thanked him again, and he waited for the beer. Later you told me he was impolite. You want to see what impolite is? Come on up, Mamma. Watch your flaccid daughter spook and puke her house to death. I am what you would call a moral lapse. I am not polite. I'm an inconsiderate girl. If I had a child when I lost my child you would tell me I'd gone to pieces. You would take my child away until I behaved. You've always wanted children. Well listen—I am a child right now. Do you know that I'm a child? Why don't you take me away? Why doesn't someone come and take me away? He sometimes drives the truck home with its plow and clears the snow away from the house. He works for the state where they have a ski tow and next door to it is where they keep fish in the summer time, and birds in big cages. He also takes care of the ducklings and the baby swans in a little house with glass walls which they keep hot so nothing dies. It's what they call a kind of preserve. The only preserve I know is red and slimy in jars. I make it out of berries and myself. But he also has to drive the truck to earn his pay. Ever hear of a poet driving a truck? He drives a truck. Like the shit-kickers who go at night without their wives to the ski lodges if they can afford the beer. You'd think the goddam beer was made out of blood, the way they charge for it. He took me to one. Polished wood and wooden tables with names the jolly people from New York City carve onto the tops. Everybody standing around and sitting around and drinking their jolly beverages in skin-tight clothes. The cunts from Manhattan up for a wedding or a sad piece of ass, whichever comes first. This girl with hair all over her face kept looking at me. I told him "There's this hairy girl over there? Can you see her? I think she thinks I'm a man." He looked at her, he looked at me, he smiled. I said "I think she thinks I'm a man." He shook his head. He said did I want another beer. I said "I want her to stop looking at me like that. Would you tell her I am not a man?" He looked at his beer and stopped smiling. I said "I'm not. I'm not!" The people she was with turned around. They looked at me as if I were a man. I said "I'm *not!*" The bar was quiet enough to die in. I closed my eyes to look inside and see if I was dead. He took me home. I don't know why. I make the house that quiet too. Why should he want to be home with me? Is that why Daddy can't come home any more? Do you think he leaves you all alone because you make his life so quiet and puzzling to be in? Mamma, do you think I'm like you? Am I dead too? Did you bear a dead little girl? Am I a ghost who's talking to you? Not talking to you. Because you bet your life, you bet my life, I'll never send this. Will I. No. *No* He doesn't send his things out either. Isn't that hard to understand? He writes poems and he keeps them here. He used to write poems. I don't know what he's writing now. Oh, yes, I wanted to tell you that the article you sent on artificial insemination was very edifying. Very enlightening. You'll understand—no you won't—that I didn't show it to him. See, he might think you were telling us his semen is faulty. He might think you were saying his balls didn't work somehow and we should try something a little more sure. But it was very considerate, Mamma. So was the clipping in your last letter, but I don't think we want to adopt any Oriental war victims this year. I think we have enough war victims this year. Jesus. You should see the war! Though a little dying between friends . . . We do have a little dying here between friends. One of his friends has a wife who *does* things. The friend drives a snowplow for the state and his wife stays home and *does* things. She called me up with an invitation to a Bee-Line party. We could all sit around, she said, and drink some instant coffee and this lady from the Bee-Line catalogue company would show us their Spring Line. Marvelous pants suits made of treated paper. Dresses you can also use for tents in case you have to bivouac on the sides of small mountains. Shoes that dissolve in wet air. And in the very latest styles right out of *Vogue!* I was very polite. I said "Are you kidding me?" I thought that was polite. I thought it was preferable to saying "I don't think I could sit and listen to you talk about your kids this year. And anyway, you're not in my class. You're the working class. I'm an intellectual kind of lady, see. I'm creative. I make things. You know, corpses and all." So instead I was polite. He didn't think I was. He didn't say so. He wouldn't. He doesn't. Do you know how much I wish he would? If you understand me, send me a clipping about manners. Send me some handy household hints from the hometown news—about reusing scouring powder, about low-phosphate douche. Send me some advice. Tell me what to do. I saw an article once called "Should You Sleep with Your Analyst?" It recommended yes and no. Which was very handy, actually. I can use some yes and no. "Should You Sleep with Your Husband?" Ha. He masturbates, Mamma. Should I tell him that his prick will fall off? Shall I tell him he'll get pimples and lose his energy? Maybe that's why he does it. Maybe he's masturbating to death. Suicide by jerking off. And let me tell you right away that, no, I am not planning to kill

21

myself. I want to live for a long time and be happy all the time and make him happier than that and we'll never not talk to each other or sometimes not remember to get into bed. I am working on that. It's my spring project. Just as soon as the weather clears. As soon as the season changes. When the light is clearer. When something besides the evergreens turns green. When anything grows. When the birds come back. When I come back. We'll plant some trees in front of the house. We'll plant some junipers and yews as hedges. Projects. We'll make our household happy again and live forever in the woods. I'll paint. I'll start by sketching. I'll sketch him in the nude. We'll both be in the nude. I'll gesso a canvas and we'll screw all over it and roll on the floors and paint the house with our sweet white asses. I'll fuck him till he's limper than a postmasturbation husband in the middle of our nights. We'll talk about his finger. I'll tell him not to call his hand a claw. We'll talk about everything. We'll have babies and live to be a hundred years old. Nothing will die. Our children will celebrate us. Write us letters from far away when we're old. Love us long distance. That's what we do now. From here to the bedroom. Bedroom to here. Here to the kitchen and back. All over the house from secret places we are sending invisible messages. SOS SOS MAYDAY MAYDAY Are you there? Who are you? Am I here? Am I? Are you? *Always, yes* Which leads us to the infidelity. Shall I tell you about it? How I was dry inside and probably smelling like old meat? How while he made love to his hand I was a whore—a necessary whore—with someone else? It was anyone else, of course. You're practical too. Our bodies make us practical, don't they, Mamma? I was simply being a good New England girl. Bad New England girl. Dried up nasty New England woman in the sack with someone who was anyone at the time. Disservice all around except to me. I was serviced. Like a car. I read a story once where a teacher said his students were cars. I always think of college as a big garage. The smell of exhaust. But what I'm trying to say, Mamma, is thank you for the mail. It's good to get your letters.

22

We live for the mail. If the rural delivery car hasn't stopped by a quarter of eight, when he has to leave to drive his truck, then he makes excuses to wait. He has to see the mail. If he can't wait, I have to telephone if there's mail. If he goes out for the mail and I wait here—I've been waiting here all winter—then he has to come upstairs, or wherever I am. If there's mail for me to read. If there isn't he doesn't have to come. Lately he hasn't. More and more we need reasons now to follow each other in the rooms of the house. I used to understand it when he was sending the poems out. I used to see why he had to have the mail. But now he doesn't send out letters filled with poems and envelopes with his name on them. He doesn't get letters back saying Yes or No. So what does he want from the mailbox? *Yes or No* And why do I want mail? I want packages in the mail. Cartons. Crates. I want thick fingers on my forehead coming from the mail. Cold hard palms on the back of my neck mailed in brown paper from Sanduskie. I want letters cut in marble, cut in ice, in granite blocks, that say WELCOME. WELCOME. HERE IS SOMETHING EASY TO DO. YOU WIN! I want the smell of strawberries fat with juices in the hottest sun. I want one sweet cold-lipped kiss on the inside of my thigh. I want one touch of tongue at the base of my spine where my buttocks begin. I almost don't have any ass left, I'm so skinny. I weigh myself to see how skinny I am. To see how terribly I disregard my body I am studying it in the few spare moments I take out from studying my mind. I dress terribly when I think about what to dress in. I think I do it on purpose. I think I do everything on purpose. I'm so skinny I don't have any chest. I don't need a bra. Not like these nipple museums, the billboards for bedwork in their après-ski tits that float in the air of the lounges, the bathrooms of motels, the minds and hearts of their countrymen. Bounce bounce wabble. I couldn't bounce there if you shook me by my ankles. Which no one, let me hasten to add, ever does. I don't get shaken much these days. I'm just flat. I look at myself in the mirrors we have. I take off my clothes if I chanced to put some on and I look at myself and I look like a boy. I never look below the waist. I have big ribs, big ribcage, but no meat on top. What do I keep in my ribcage, Mamma? Leopards and pigs. The leopards are killing the pigs in my cage. You know what I can't finish any of? Novels. Novelists come on so glib. I'm only reading serious things from now on. Where they don't take somebody's mind and slice it and wrap it up and serve it to you. And then they go on television to talk to somebody about art who thinks art is the name of the guy who's laying his wife. They talk about hard work. They say purpose. They tell us about their searing emotions. Empathy for the suffering of. I watch them. I sneer and I watch them. I watch the commercials. I watch the programs that come on after the news—shots of starving children—and I watch reruns of programs where right-wing cops stop drug fiends from polluting America. I watch left-wing detectives get hit on the head in disguise and then stop spies from selling us out to unnamed Powers. I watch cowboys' wives getting raped by Indians who are white men or white men who are Indians. I watch queers get blackmailed in Hawaii by the sinister Chinese. I watch ladies on commercials in between. Every four to eight minutes I watch ladies on commercials in between. They are dutiful, hard-working, earnest and kind. They serve their children well. They service their husbands as if they were cars. They vow to do their laundry better. Sometimes they get colds and their husbands (played by men afraid of flesh) touch their foreheads with frightened fingers and give them patent medicines that get them out of bed so they put dinner made of soybean and sodium glutamate down on the table before the hungry husband's home from work. I see mothers buying better diapers for their infants. I see infants not getting troubled with air in their bottle. I see children rescued from the pain of cuts and bruises. I see mothers trading secrets on child care as their elevator plunges in place. I see the last news of the night—shots of starving children—and I see the signals from Manchester and Boston, hear the final high hum which means it's time to read. There's nothing to read but novels and poems. I don't read novels any more. And there's no one writing poems. Sometimes I sleep in the living room in front of the set. Sometimes I turn off the set. Sometimes I go upstairs and sleep beside him. Sometimes I come up here and sleep. Sometimes I don't sleep downstairs or here or in the bed with him. I lie in all of those places from time to time, not sleeping. Sometimes I walk around. Or stand at this window and look out on snow falling, or snow that's settled in, and wait for the sound of a car and listen to that, then see the brightness of lights in the air and wait and see the car coming and going away, the lights dying, the sound falling into the snow like ink into soft paper, then stand here with nothing to wait for. Sometimes I look with the lights on at my face in the black window. I take off my clothes and look at myself from the waist to the throat and I look like a boy. And what does Daddy do when he doesn't come to bed? And you? I tell myself I'll miss you when you're dead. I tell myself how guilty I feel. Often it feels like you're dead and I only sometimes feel sad. We have a friend we always write to. Sometimes he visits us. He's the saddest crazy man. Like brittle glass. He has no wife. She has their kids. He has no kids. He mourns them. He came here during the winter that's supposed to be ending. It's February and the winter won't end. It's nearly March and nothing good has happened to the world. Every morning we see that it snowed in the night. It's like a curse. Every morning it's supposed to be getting better, but it's snowed. We get visited by our white blight while we're sleeping. We get up and we see that we're cursed. I keep thinking that if I go to bed on time and get up late there won't be any snow. Brown mud. Roots and bugs and heat all over. But I don't go to bed on time. I don't go with him when he goes. And he's so gorgeous every night: "Okay, babe. I'm bushed, I'm going up." Wait for me. Wait for me. "Get some sleep, babe. Love you. Sleep tight. Get some sleep." Wait for me. Mamma, do you purse your lips when you go alone to your bedroom? All he does is go. All

25

I do is stay. I don't know what to do for him. He doesn't purse his lips. His face is blank as a baby's when it sleeps. February twenty-nine, the end of the month is one day later than the end of the month. If I drive today to the village and smile at the one-armed grocer and buy a newspaper every other page will have a small one-inch item at the end of every article on famine and desire. It will tell about the leap year gift, an extra day in the second month. Something about stars. About the astronomical year, which is three hundred and sixty-five and one quarter days long. Our calendars lack the quarter. Our calendars give no quarter. So we take it for ourselves. Every four years we seize a day. I open my hand in front of the window and squeeze my black-stained fingers shut. Below me on the slanting roof I see the tops of icicles. Below, in the living room, if I were there—if he were there— one of us could look out the living room window and see thick bars of ice from the low roof's edges hang down to nearly the ground. If I drove into town I'd be riding westward coming back. Driving into the sun, I would squint and feel sleepy. Pitch off the road and start rolling slow as a movie, where you feel no motion, only see signals. Feel no pain. You hear its sounds. I would roll so slowly. Like a woodchip off an ax I would lodge in a snowmound at the trunk of a giant round tree. The car would be soft as my body. I would huddle at the tree's thick-rooted base. I would sleep until I stopped breathing. I would rise like the woodchip falling slowly in reverse. I would keep on rising. I would fall upon the house and melt through the roof to stand beside his bed. I would tell him things. He would fail to understand me. I would tell him "But I'm trying so hard!" Like the movie in reverse again I would fall away up into the air and descend again beside you, Mamma. I would tell you things. You would fail to understand me. I would call to you: "Mamma! Mamma!" *Mamma* This is clearly decline. I am very clearly going into decline. A hundred years ago they'd have called it brain fever. Progress! Now I *have* brain fever and they don't use the words any more.

26

They say headache. Well listen, medical science, technological warfare experts, crooks in white smocks at the AMA, I no longer have headaches. I have fever of the brain. My cells are swollen. There is pus draining into my eyes. I suck on aspirin between my teeth. I place them under my tongue. I let them dissolve in every orifice. I bathe in solutions of aspirin and bile. A headache is what a female fruit fly has when she gets her period. I have *pain!* Fine, take two aspirin and try to relax. You'll feel better when you relax. Yes. Thank you doctor. I'll send you a breast in the morning. Yes. Listen, I have a husband who used to write poems. He used to teach school and he used to write poems and he used to love me in the morning when I'd worry that my mouth tasted to him like what it tasted to me. That was the taste that he wanted. And the taste of him, he wanted to suck that off the inside of my lower lip. Can you see the chain of days? From the first time to here in the crotch of New Hampshire. From the summer into autumn into winter into now, February ending, the spring alleged to begin. And him, walking down along that chain, too cold to touch nearly, made of thick steel, ice-covered, infinite. Him walking down along it. Touching as much as he can. What if he stopped and planted those legs and sweated and shook and ripped it apart like a chain made of paper by children in school? What would I do, I wonder. He goes to work in a truck. He comes home. We talk. He touches me on the arms, on the back of my neck, the small of my back, all bony. He never touches my legs. Or my belly. Or breasts (as if I had some). I've got biceps like a dyke. I've got arms as long as his, nearly. I've got hair on my forearms and two black hairs too tiny to see on my chest. But, as they say in the trade, no tits. He doesn't touch there anyway. He wouldn't if I had a set like you, Mamma. It's all in safe places. I rub his shoulders sometimes if he's tired from driving the plow all day. Then I stop. Our kitchen is L-shaped, and the small side of the angle is where I keep the filthy dishes until he washes them. At least that hasn't changed. The other

27

side is where we eat, and where we have a little fireplace he built out of fire-brick stolen from the Swiss Fondue Chalet they were building when we moved here. We used to sit there in two decrepit rockers we bought in Boston for too much. We used to rock. He called me Ma Kettle. He wanted to cover the walls with barn siding. I told him I'd feel like a cow. He said that cows had teats. When I was pregnant again he took some siding off the inside of the barn and stacked it inside. It's still there. Behind the house is the little porch and then the field and brush and his thumb. He still holds his hand in his pocket too much.

"Too much for what?" he said.

"Too much, that's all."

"Well you just can't have *too much*. It's a measurement. What are you measuring against? Too much for what?"

"For me. Okay, then? For me."

"All right. Suppose I hang it out."

"Fine."

"All right?"

"I said fine."

"Babe, you were the one who brought it up."

"I didn't know we'd have a discussion."

"What's wrong with a discussion, babe?"

"What we're discussing."

"All right. What shall we talk about?"

"I don't know."

"I mean what interests you these days? What are you reading? Are you sketching? Painting? Having fun?"

"That wasn't hilarious."

"I know."

"That was dumb."

"I know."

"So why did you say it?"

"Babe, are we having a fight?"

"Yes. No."

"What—I have a choice?"

28

"Yes."

"Of what?"

"Nothing. Nothing."

And so to bed. Beds. And nighttime. Morning. Afternoon. Another night. The old New England carousel. The wooden horses pumping up and down, around, the wobbly circles day and night, the sun a part of the carousel, the moon, the house and road and cars gone by and mail truck going past and coming back to go past again back into the village and the wooden post office, the shadows of trees, the crystals of ice in the sun, the icicles that sometimes drip, and him, and me, and bed, and beds. The not reading novels. The not writing poems. The never painting. The ink on my fingers. My face in the blackened window at night looking in on me. Mamma, where do you look from at night? What do you stare at? Where does Daddy sleep? Where was he sleeping when I came back home, eighteen, devirginized, sick a little, disappointed, maybe sad, too bruised to be worried, too bored somewhere inside the headache I was growing for the fear of what you'd think, what Daddy would think, what my date—he was a soldier, and he died—would think if he learned to think which he didn't? And where is Daddy now? We have this friend, Mamma. A kind of scholar. He wrote a book. He lost his children and his wife. They left him alone. He wrote his book because they left him alone. When he was done with the writing he looked around and they still weren't there. He went looking—first for them, then for anything else. Well what are friends for if not for anything else? He stayed here a while. Then he left. He went back home, and we stayed here. We stay here now. We're confused. He writes to us and we write back. He's confused. My husband drives a truck for the state and doesn't write poems. I write you letters I don't send. Our friend doesn't work on a book. The spring doesn't come. The ice doesn't melt. And what I wonder is what I should do if the spring does come. When the ice melts if it does, and it will, maybe. If the ice ever melts I wonder what I should do.

29

Mamma, what will you do? What are you doing now? My husband is driving a truck. I tore a piece of newsprint into a little shape and wrote the little lines onto it, put it where he sits for coffee and bread before he goes to work.

> Westron wind, when will thou blow?
> The small rain down can rain.
> Christ, that my love were in my arms,
> And I in my bed again.

He was wearing his corduroys and the big woolly shirt of red and black squares, an insulated vest. He looked at the words and smiled. He had those smile wrinkles at his eyes and around his mouth. His forehead was furrowed. He put the page face down, and I stood at the electric percolator, not pouring, just standing to wait.

He said "Western Wind. The title—"

"Yup. A little research by the old lady."

"It's sweet, isn't it. I mean, it's a very sad poem. And sweet. You were sweet to give it to me."

"I like it" I said.

"Sweet" he said.

"You make it sound like a candy bar."

"No, I don't mean to. I mean thank you."

"I hate for you to thank me. But I do wish the goddam spring would come. Don't you?"

"Yeah. Yeah. Could I have some of that coffee? Would you sit down and have some too?"

So we sat there like a married couple. He looked at me like a boy trying to pick up a girl. Which is how the army de-virginizer did it, matter of fact. We looked at our coffee and the bread we didn't toast. I watched him when he wasn't looking at me. He looked when he thought I wasn't watching. He folded his napkin with his whole hand, the fingers moving like animals—half in length, then half in width, then half of that, then half the length of that, the width of what was left, then almost gone. I put my head down on my arms and he said "Are you crying?"

I nodded my head.

He said "You'll look like a lizard when you're finished. You always look terrible."

I nodded my head. I couldn't stop.

He said "Babe—what shall I do?"

I couldn't tell him. I couldn't stop.

"Babe?"

"Mmf."

"Honey?"

"Oh, God, no, yes, I don't know. Those are the only answers. I don't know which one. What are you asking?"

"Can't we help each other out a little?"

I went back down to my arms again. I couldn't stop.

He stood up and then he stood behind me. He touched me on the head with his hands. As if my head were a vessel that would spill. We stayed like that. He went to work. Later the telephone rang and I didn't answer it. The mail car came and I didn't go out. I took the newsprint back and brought it up here. It's someplace in the room. So am I. The western wind, slow rain. *Us* We're moving into March now. We're a couple of days into March. How do you like my letter so far? I should write it in red. Oh yes the scarlet letter. Aha. In black we can call it the black letter. Does that do anything for you? What would you call an unmailed letter that's black? You could call it me if you wanted. Daughter. Your unmailed letter sincerely. *Us* I wonder what I would do if we had a child. See? Still "we." It isn't lost. We aren't lost. If the period goes in the right place next to we we aren't lost. The placement of my periods is what I'm all about. I get so tired of living from one bloody passage to the next. I'm a clock made of tissues that ooze. So are you. He hates my periods, he always did. When we first got married I thought he was a full-time assman, he jumped all over me so hard so much. He was so big and full of balls. It turned out that he used to screw before me but

31

he was scared. In all nine years he never really told me why. I think I know. We have a tenth anniversary coming. I wonder what we'll do. He used to screw but he never knew what he was doing. He was scared of their cunts, I think. There was always something wrong with them in the one or two or three little stories he'd tell. One would smell bad. The other was too big. Always the place he'd disappear into, that's what scared him. I think he was always afraid he wouldn't come back. He'd get lost. Like the jokes. Bad jokes. Six-foot-four of sad bad joke. There was always something wrong. They'd end up blowing him. His favorite sport, getting blown before a game because the coach said stay pure. I think he wanted to stay pure. Always. He's even afraid of cellars that are dark and wet and deep. But he could never listen to anyone. He couldn't take an order. I love that. So he would get blown by a campus queenlet and then shoot a thousand baskets and get drunk with the basketball studs. Why not? Why not be a boy? Boys like to look at the junior high school homeroom president girls and search their faces for pimples. Extra armpit sweat that stains the blouse. Imagined smells. They ferret out menstruation signs like dogs. Because they're scared of it all. Like him. He wouldn't touch me when I bled. Unless I was losing a baby, of course. He was fine about that. But he did learn how to make love. He could keep me up for an hour it felt like. He learned to relax pretty much. One thing about being childless, you can do it in the afternoons. Backyards at teatime. In between drinks. As hors d'oeuvres. We're lucky. Ex-boyfriend to husband screwing ex-boyfriend's lay, now a wife: "Hey, buddy. Lots of room in there, huh?" Husband: "Plenty. So?" "Well if you find a motorbike up there, it's mine." Lots of room. Lots of mucous membrane rapidly drying from lack of use. I don't have to use it much to come. I've done that. I hate it. I feel worse. It's worse than being unfaithful. Maybe it is unfaithful. Not if he does it. God knows he probably should. He has to. If he doesn't have to, he should. Why should he be faithful to me? I'm not. I wonder what I would do if I had a

child. Die, most likely. And if I didn't? Would it be like on TV?
Like my roommates from school? All bows and laces, clean-
smelling laundry? Powder and delight? Would I lie in a summer meadow and hold him over my head between the sun and
me and laugh? Would he laugh back? It would have to be a he.
Boys are the most beautiful. The most vulnerable, fragile,
they need you the most. Baby girls are like cats. Boys are like
puppies. They need you the most. Poor Mamma, you had girls.
And now what do you have? Nothing. Nothing. Me. I used to
think a baby would disturb our lives. Look what he'd disturb.
What we wouldn't have is this. So let's have a baby. Yes. Let's
get out the old graphs, the old thermometer. It's a new form
of sex. The husband sticks a thermometer up the rectum of his
wife. They wait. They read the chart. They enter their data.
They screw on time, by the numbers. They wait. She bleeds.
She cries. They say oh next time. And they stick the glass and
mercury up her ass. They read the numbers off and write them
down. They screw on time. She bleeds. This time they both cry.
Then they both make jokes. They say oh next time. Then
they stick and read and write and screw and bleed and cry and
another month has passed. They turn into clocks that screw
instead of ticking. They spend their lives like that. They sometimes forget that they're loving. They act like they're working
on something for someone. They become each other's office.
Every night they go to work. He wears a tie to bed. He shines
his shoes while she douches. He punches her in like a clock. In
the morning they take her temperature and write the numbers
down. Her ovaries ache. She bleeds and has cramps. They take
turns weeping. Then one day they turn away from one another
because he's embarrassed. In the bathroom he masturbates into
a sterile vial. Sterile and vile, he says. They have a fight. They
drive to the county clinic and drop his drops off. They go to the
doctor in a week and he tells them maybe yes and no. They go
to her doctor and she lies with her legs up in stirrups and cries.
He explores her like a bear reaching in for food. He tells her
maybe yes and no. They go home and have a drink. They have

33

another drink and some more. The sun crawls across their living room floor and he says he'll quit his job. They'll go away. She says to where? From what? They have another drink. The sun is reaching across the floor like an animal searching for food. They move away. They take a house. He takes a job. She forgets to unpack her paints. He loses a thumb. She loses a life. Her mother writes that babies are raining on the neighborhood. One girl got pregnant and killed herself. She writes back to her mother "So did I." She places the period next to the I. It is like that through the winter. Then it is spring, except spring doesn't come. He says in the spring they'll plant a fruit tree in the front yard. She asks him if that's not very self-conscious. He says yes. He says so what. They have a fight. The snow lies everywhere and falls each night. A wandering ruined friend comes to call. They comfort him. He leaves. No one is comforted. On television everyone is comforted. In an hour or an hour and a half, everyone is comforted. There is a rule on television that everyone who deserves it by virtue of being pretty or strong, or informing for the FBI, must be allotted his comfort. And comfort must come by the end of the show. Peace is a factor of time. Time is measured by the doling out of tidings that make people glad. At the end of the broadcasting night there are no programs. So there is no peace. Nor is there time. There's a high endless hum in which everyone dies or is tortured. During that time you're requested to sleep. I stay awake and watch it all. I do not benefit from that secret observation. I learn nothing. Nothing changes in my life. I wonder if I'm enjoying myself. Mamma, that's what scares me most. I'm getting habituated. I'm a frightening drug. I'm my addict. What would happen if I ran out of paper? Would I stop? Would I sit here with no one to talk to? Would I stop staying up here so much? Would I stop listening to my voice? Stop making catalogues of grief? No. I would write until the ink ran out. On the walls and floors and ceiling. On the bedspread and the quilt, the sheets and mattress. On the steel of the bedsprings. I would jam the pen against the windows until

34

they broke. I would write on my body. Carve the pen point into my tongue. Write with my blood on the ink that I wrote on the walls with. If I died because I poisoned myself with my own inky words I would twitch all my fear and perversion at the doctor until my nerves and muscles stopped working. Blink my eyes in secret messages I understood until nothing could move. If I died I would go on. *Yes* In fact I might have died. Who would argue with a grieving woman? Who would tell me I'm alive? I don't want to die. I want to live like a person in a house with a husband. I want us to be glad all the time. I don't want him living without me. I don't want him sad without me and then happy without me. Not without me. We're in this together. Because we love each other we can't be happy alone and be fair. So there is no hope if you love. Doctor Death's Daily Dose. Write this in your notebooks and turn yourself in at the end of the term. A marriage is a terminal disease. Unless it's televised. Then it ends after the late news and sometimes a little sermon, the airplanes dropping bombs for peace and the flag that waves in atomic winds. Then in the morning it begins again unless you don't go to sleep. In which case it goes on. Love. The prison. Everything comes down to cells. Like the time we went to England and they arrested us. So politely in Salisbury, England. Driving an unregistered car. And in the plastic police station, those tough men being polite, me being scared, him red and raging.

"Now, sir, will you tell us again why your vehicle wasn't properly registered."

"Because they wouldn't register me in London."

"Yes sir. But this is Wiltshire County, sir. You'd have to register your vehicle—Austin, is it? Ah: the eighteen hundred, a lovely car—you'd have to register with the County Council in Trowbridge, that'd be. So they were quite correct not registering you in London. You must have told them you were letting the cottage in Wiltshire."

"Yes."

"So you see, they were quite correct."

"Except I bought the goddam car in London."

"Easy on, sir, easy on now. Yes. But if you weren't about to *operate* the vehicle—it's all in where you operate, you see—not going to actually *run* the car in London, why, then, they'd no choice but to turn you down, now, had they?"

"Okay."

"Sir?"

"I said okay. I believe you. I believe *them*."

"Well, then—"

"Except I had to get here, didn't I?"

"Quite correct."

"I couldn't take the train up and let the car drive itself or take a boat to Southampton and walk or something, could I?"

"Ah."

"So I drove it here. If you'll ask one of the troopers here to check the glove compartment—"

"Sir?"

"Check the fucking *boot*. There's a map there. Trowbridge is circled in red pen. We were going to Trowbridge to register the—"

"Easy on. We can settle this, I think, without losing tempers. Don't you think?"

"So I'm illegal until I get legal. But the legal people wouldn't let me get legal. They *made* me illegal. Now you're arresting us for *being* illegal. You won't let me go *make* us legal. That's why I'm losing my temper. Understand?"

"Of course, I understand, sir. It happens all the time."

"Oh Jesus. That's how it's supposed to work, huh?"

"The system does have its shortcomings, sir."

"One of which would be the entire system?"

"Ah. Well, more or less, in this case, I would say."

"Would you?"

"I don't want to have to detain you, sir."

"Then why don't you let us go?"

"Actually, I'm required—"

36

"To detain us."

"Yes."

We slept that night in the Red Lion on a fifteenth-century bed that had gargoyles and bishops carved into the posts. Softest mattress invented. We were shaped like bowls of flesh, it sagged so much in the middle. We screwed three times and slept all day. We registered our car. We registered ourselves on the bed. We saw the statues of dead knights in the Salisbury Cathedral and stood outside and stared at the spire. It didn't stop. We didn't stop. There were no dead nights. We read novels and painted and read and wrote poems. We lived in a cottage that was thatched and made of brick and flint. We were married and married and married. The English never let their children talk. A little boy in shorts bumped into me in Wilton; I apologized. His father cracked him in the side of the face with the side of his hand. He said "Watch where you go." He waited to see if he cried. He walked away. Before he followed him, the boy watched him go. He wept as soon as his father's back was turned. I would let my baby talk. But I would hit him. I know I would hit him. When haven't I struck? That boy in Wilton—he never said a syllable. He didn't make noise when he cried. Cry means *cry!* My husband is silent. He crouches in a cup over the wheel of a big orange truck with lots of wheels and chains and a plow in front that's as high as the prow of a boat, a plow on the right-hand side that's smaller to push what the big plow plows, and sand falls off the back of the truck to give the world some traction. He stares straight ahead. The yellow light on top of the cab turns around. Sometimes they call him on the radio and he goes where they tell him. Pushing the snow. Winds blow the tops of the snow banks off and the clouds go gritting across the windshield. Sometimes for half a mile he doesn't see. He knows the road. He's lucky. He's in danger. He doesn't care. And sometimes winds pull the bottoms of the banks and blow them across the road like little streams that don't stop. He gets hypnotized, watching them. His hands know the way. Other-

wise he'd have an accident and plow off the road. Open a new
road through embankments and fences and trees. Bleeding on
the snow. He doesn't care. Mamma, do you know how much he
remembers from when he was a kid? He remembers rationing
stamps when his mother first got them and air raids in an apartment house some place and the vets who sold war bonds. He
remembers when he was two and three. I can't remember anything. I can't remember much. I remember in Peter Pan Nur-
sery School they told us to eat the potatoes because we would
grow up strong. I didn't want to grow up strong. I wanted to be
outside. I could smell the mildewed rag they wiped the tables
with. Everything smelled like vomit. I said no. They held my
nose and pushed the potatoes in with a ladle. I opened a window that was open a little bit. I stuck my head and shoulders in
and pushed my way through. They heard the window squeak-
ing and pulled me in. I threw up in the giant box of rock salt
they let us play in if we were good. I was never good again and
I didn't go back. You hired a maid. You told me that she
loved me after she died. I remember that. I don't remember
her. I remember when you were having Cassie in the hospital. I don't remember when you went there. I remember you
were not in the house. I think of you with your chestnut hair
pulled out of its bun on a pillow. But I don't remember you. I
remember Daddy coming home. I hid in the dining room. The
sun was bright and buttery all over. He walked into the living
room. God it feels so big! What huge rooms they are when I
remember them! He carried a balloon he bought at the station.
It was Mickey Mouse's head. The ears stuck up. The face
was floating in the air. It was summer and Daddy wore his
seersucker suit with stripes. He put the string in my hand and
we went to the hospital. The face came with me. Did anyone
take care of me while I waited in the waiting room? He loved
me so much. He would have had a nurse take care of me. Now
they don't take care of you. Sometimes they cry. But they
really can't take care of me. When I took him to the hospital
I had to wait outside the emergency room. I tried to sit down.

38

He went away. I couldn't sit because of the cramps. So I went home. I wonder what they thought of me. When I came back next morning they disapproved until I told them I had sat all night. Doing a little bleeding, I said. I smiled my brave smile. Then I screamed at them and the young nurse cried. Her eyes ran down her face. But they couldn't take care of me. He came out with his hand holding his hand. You came home with a baby. I came home with his hand. There are evening grosbeaks all over the fence this morning. They sound upset, which is anthropomorphism. The light is lighter. A little frost has gone out of the wind. It's bound to be spring soon. We're putting our money on spring. We keep speaking of spring. But we don't know what to say. I wonder what we're hoping for. A letter came from Daddy yesterday. He mailed it from his office. How long has it been since you went to his office? I know it's big but it keeps feeling tiny. Every time he writes I think his office is small. Because he mails these memo sheets from his office. They're like his letterhead but tiny. Little reduced replicas of his big paper, and he writes on them with his tiny slanting words. So small I can hardly read them. He puts a hundred words in black on the little white sheet. I have to study what he says. He makes jokes. He says he's busy. He has this client in Germany and he keeps flying there. Then his client flies here. They have dinner and talk. They work all night. A German engineer works with them. He doesn't trust the engineer. He thinks he's a spy. Because of this building in Germany that collapsed. And American investments. International deals, he says. He doesn't trust the engineer. He doesn't trust his client. He doesn't even trust himself, he says. That's when I see his big sweet ugly smile. And Mickey Mouse who floated behind me on a string. The sunlight in our house. He says that you're fine. Are you fine, Mamma? He sends me his love. He wishes we could see each other. That's what we say about spring. We send these tiny little messages about March which is followed by April. When we study them they say we wish we could see each other. We are waiting. I am in my

39

waiting room. This morning I took four aspirin. I'm immune. This morning he went to work, as he always does. It snowed a little last night, but not enough to plow. Today he'll do other things. He'll check the birds. They'll carry lumber in a truck. Pick up fencing and put it someplace. Children will come with their teacher from school and he'll show them around. He'll point to the animals. The children will giggle and talk of the smell. He'll talk about pollution, conservation, erosion, restocking. The teacher will tell them to listen. They won't. He'll drink coffee with the other men. They'll talk about the basketball game on television. Will Boston win this year? He'll say yes. Someone will say no. A secretary with tits will stand in a window and look at them. They'll look back. Someone will growl and they'll all say something about getting into her. The three men who did will smile. He will not write poems. When he was in college and doing construction work he talked his poems to himself. He worked on the streets in Roxbury. Digging sewers for a housing project. Shoveling dirt for lawns and raking the rocks out. At night he would drink beer and write poems. On the job he would always remember the poems and say them to himself. He would shovel and pull on his rake and walk his wheelbarrow to the rhythm of his poems. He would write his poems to the rhythm of his rake. We went to a bar one night, the three of us. We were comforting each other. Baker when he came to us in mourning for his wife and kids. Especially kids. He used amphetamines to drive up from New York. He couldn't calm down. When he drove home we didn't talk about him any more. He stopped being named in our house. But while he was, we went to a bar. We talked about nothing. We started out talking about everything and then we couldn't talk. It was an old hotel with the parlor torn out so that we walked into a long narrow room that was dark with a bar at the far end. A little corner room was for a band. Seven screaming maniacs with jiggling balls all wired and plugged into electric boxes and electric guitars and electric fiddles and a hundred drums. They banged and shrieked. The darkness was a soft balloon their sound kept pushing out of shape. There were people at tables and people at the bar. The man behind the bar wore a pistol in a holster. Baker said "Is this a dangerous place?"

I said "Only if you're suspected of being human. Otherwise they leave you alone." I said "Would you get us a lot to drink, honey?" and Phil went to the bar. Big enough for no one to bother him. For the country-type hookers to look him up and down a couple of times and think.

Baker said "Holy jumping God. Is this where you guys always go?"

"I never came here before." They were looking at him. One of them talked to him and he smiled. She cupped her hands and said something funny and they laughed. Her hands kept moving back toward her. He looked as if he knew where the hands were going.

Baker said "We gotta have a good time tonight."

I said "When was the last time you had a good time?"

"Berkeley. Nineteen-sixty-two."

"You are a shmuck."

"Right. Right. Listen, we must have a fantastic time tonight. This is one of those imperative nights when you got to have a good time." His eyes were jumping inside his black-rimmed glasses like the music. He was skinny and flat and I could see the artery in his throat jumping. He folded and kneaded his hands. They kept moving. His hair stood straight up. Pulled by electric currents. He looked flooded with static. He couldn't sit still. He said "I keep on thinking about you guys. I feel bad for you guys and you have a place like this. You come here a lot? You must be up to your ass in crazy times, right?"

I said "I never came here before. He comes here. I don't know when. This is where *he* comes. I stay home pretty much these days."

"Yeah. Yeah, you do. You told me, didn't you? I can't remember."

"What?"

"I can't remember things."

"Well look what you—look at the goddam pills you're always popping. No wonder."

"No wonder. Right. You know you wrote me two letters in a year? And one was so crazy—"

"This wasn't our best year."

"Right. Listen. Better years are on their way."

"You know this?"

"What?"

"Come on, Baker, shmuck. Pay attention to me!"

"Oh, listen. If you knew the attention I pay to you. All the time. I'm paying so much attention to you—why don't we get married. You remember when I wanted you to marry me?"

"You always want me to marry you."

"That's true."

"Big deal."

"Big deal. You come here a lot? This is a crazy place." Phil left her. The music changed and he left her and came over with a pitcher of beer and glasses. Baker said "I was proposing marriage. I made a decent proposal and she scorned me."

He sat down and nodded, grinned, poured beer, looked at something in the room, stopped grinning, looked at his beer. He said "I did the same myself."

"Recently?" Baker said.

"Always" he said.

Baker said "Booooooo. Bad tidings. Listen, I am in *love* with you two guys. Right?"

He said "Right. Right. But you're always in love with someone."

"Hey" Baker said. "No, bad—I mean *you*. I'm a serious man, hey. Right? I'm talking about love. I'm saying this *straight*. Now listen: I love you."

He said "We do too, Baker. We love you and we love us and we love everybody. And everyone loves us."

The screaming kids were playing "Turkey in the Straw."

42

Girls were bouncing around in ski pants and people were hooking each other's arms. Nobody made a square. Nobody could. The shapes kept melting. The man with the pistol watched us all. People on the floor kept moving around into shapes that melted. Baker was thumping a leg up and down. There was more beer and people too drunk to dance and the hooker at the bar was staring. Baker stood up and sat down. He said "Must pee. *Have* to pee. Or dance. Hey, I have to pee and frolic and I can't decide."

The one from the bar came over in six different maneuvers, like a fat boat in cross winds. Her big tits rang like bells. Up and down, up and down. Baker said "Are you my wife?"

She said, "I'm your *life.*"

Baker looked at us, his eyes jumping up and down with her chest. He said "I am called." He told her "Listen, I have this problem." He put an arm around her, one hand on a breast, and whispered. He whispered more and she moved herself into his hand. She giggled and butted her head up into his face. She whispered back. He said "All *right!*" She stuck her fingers into the top of his white dungarees and towed him behind her toward the bar. Tug with a bouncing barge. The shapes kept melting. The music went on. Like his eyes. She looked back at us. We were drinking and not looking at each other.

I said "This is sad."

He turned around and leaned his forehead on my arm. He said "I think he's finished."

"Because of her?"

"No. She doesn't finish anything."

"What's *that* supposed to mean."

"Nothing. Like her. Nothing. I mean him—he's terrible. I don't know who he is. He doesn't know who we are."

"Like us."

"Huh?"

"You know."

"Oh. Sort of. Yes. I guess I sort of do. Except I don't think we're finished."

"No. But we're sad."

He said "Yes. Boy, we really are."

I put my head down and kissed the top of his head. He moved it, and my face went on down to my arm. I said "Don't you wish we were fine? Really good?"

He said "We will be."

"When?"

"We'll be all right."

The shot went over the room. Like lights going on. I watched the sound move toward us. Everybody stopped. Baker was on his knees. He was holding onto a bar stool. The hooker was very calm. She was watching. She liked what she saw. The man behind the bar was pointing his gun in the air. My ears were hurting from the sound that stopped. Everything felt emptied out. Baker said "Am I dead?" The room filled up with laughter. All this noise coming back. I hid behind it and watched the man at the bar put his gun away. The band was waiting to start. They were all laughing. We stayed where we were. We held each other's hand.

Baker said "Did anybody answer me?"

The hooker said "Hey, what can I say?"

"Did I die? Did he shoot me?"

She said "Hey, you forgot to pay the man. Like it's a *rule:* you don't pay, he fires away."

The laughter came up again. And the music. More of it. People went back to dancing. Thumping in and out of shapes on the wooden floor. I saw Baker's head come up. His eyes were closed. His glasses were under the stool. His face was filled with tears. I saw his mouth move. His words were lost in the music. I saw his mouth keep moving. It said "No. Am I dead?"

At Grandma's funeral Daddy never cried. He held Aunt Ellen on his chest like a baby. His arms could have gone around her twice, she was so small. She cried into the hard twill of his suit. I did too when I was little. He pushed his chin down onto her head and watched them throw the powdery

44

dirt. The first time it sounded like chains. Each time the dirt
fell his mouth gripped harder on the noise he wanted to make.
I stood next to him and he forgot me. I said "Oh Daddy" once
and then I said nothing. He heard me saying nothing. He
thanked me later on. You stayed home with Cassie. You cried
when we were alone. Daddy held you too. No one held him.
Nobody does. Unless. Unless. What do you say, Mamma? Does
Daddy do it on the side? Think he's got a bad apartment in
New York? A Yorkville boudoir? With some soft lady wearing
velveteen? Or is he alone the way I think he is? I wonder
if he eats his dinner alone when he can't come home at night.
In restaurants with his *New York Times* propped up on the
basket of hot frozen bread. Eating the fish for his health, dry,
with no sauce. Drinking no wine. No coffee or dessert and
nothing to smoke. A dry dinner and falling asleep in a smelly
hotel that might as well be on the Cromwell Road in London
where we slept our first night there. Our room was above an
all-night garage for exhaust addicts. They slammed their overhead doors up and down. When they rolled they sounded like
grave dirt pattering down. They revved their engines, then
stopped. Revved and stopped. The motors bellowed like people
who were crazy. We were so tired. We lay in one bed and that
was too small. We lay in the separate beds they had given
us and said "So this is London. So this is London." I said "So
this is swinging London" and the motors yelled and we giggled
until we slept. When we awakened a girl who spoke no English
brought us tea. Phil said *Hasta diablo* and I spat my tea all
over the rose-pattern quilt. That poor little immigrant girl who
thought we were mad. Spitting out free tea in a language that
made no sense. Diablo. What the hell. In the cottage we rented
near Stonehenge. He said it was druids. I said it was put up
for Tess of the d'Urbervilles to lie there while the posse rode
up at dawn. When I believed what novels said. Of course it
wasn't either one. It's all quite scientific now. Observatory or
clock or something like that. Something very useful and dull.
Now I say it's rocks. Big rocks. In the cottage with a newly

thatched roof and apple trees in the backyard. Hedges all around. A giant bush that was shaped like a pear. Someone trained it that way. And the old black wooden floors. The kitchen's floor made of brick. Old furniture and a hundred thin blankets to lie beneath when it was so cold at night we couldn't read or listen to the news at ten o'clock. Early to bed. Early to rise. Rising into me like bad news a stranger slowly announced. Like baby Sam being conceived in time for us to come back home and lose him and moving up here and losing the one we never had nerve to name in advance and losing a thumb, a household, the peace we wore like comfortable clothes. The cottage on a road a dozen cars maybe traveled each day. Surrounded by hedges and old trees. And walking across the road to look down our hill to the Salisbury Plain that just kept going on. Flat forever, horizon as big as the world. The sky came all the way down. And the Golden Pheasant Inn. Some famous English writer left his wife and lived there. Some famous lion left a zoo and killed a coachman there a hundred years ago. The A30 going into London one way and Salisbury the other, passing Porton Down. He asked the landlady when she showed us the place if Porton wasn't famous. She said "Oh yes. They do all the poison gas there, you know." We stared at her and laughed. She said "But you needn't worry. They're always very quiet." He went to a little greengrocer in our tiny town there and saw a crate of lemons from Spain. He said aren't they big lemons. She looked at his face and said "Yes, nice and Jewish, aren't they?" Then she said *juicy* and went out back and her sixty-year-old daughter came in to do the rest. She never could face us again. The first thing you asked, Mamma. "Are you marrying a Jew?" I said no, of course not, never. "One-armed nigger with a stripe down his face" I told you. Phil Sorenson. My husband, the non-Semitic Jew. We should have stayed in England. Isn't that what they say about Americans? Everything would have been all right if they had stayed in England? We should have stayed there. But we came here. Like colonists. We came to New England. We chopped

46

down trees and brush. Every place we went was some frontier that we kept crossing. And now I'm the witch in the forest.

> There once was a couple in Eden
> Whose offspring emerged always bleeding.
> They buried them deep
> And then Eve went to sleep.
> She thought dreams gave her what she was needing.

Which they do not. I take aspirin and I fall asleep when I'm not tired. I dream about my headaches. I think I hear infants crying. It's the same when I wake up. When I wake up I dream that infants hear me cry. *We hear you cry* So if I write poems how come Mister Philip Sorenson the famous non-Jewish poet doesn't write them? He drives a truck and raises baby birds. He works for the state. He doesn't mention poetry. Or graves. Or Baker with his pill-head failing laugh. All the roads are black now. Brown water bleeds from the snowbanks and runs down the road like rivers. Snow falls at night but it melts in the morning and the spring is almost here in early March. Maybe we'll get lucky this year. And maybe I'll grow up. *We are trying to tell you nothing we are* Just grow. Springtime in the kitchen with our old spring chicken, Mamma. What the hell. Pots of boiling water, celery stewing, little plastic-topped bottles of herbs from impossible places, the skins of onions lying on the floor like autumn leaves. On the radio, what else but telephoned conversations from lost women and out-of-work mill hands? And who talks back to them but college dropouts with voices that come from their diaphragms? Voices coming in from impossible places. Me in the kitchen with wine for stewing chicken and wine in my beer glass. Wine that runs down my chin like the brown mud rivers that run in the road. A little sexy dinner for our wandering boy. Yes. Except the way they give you stewing chickens. Drunk on wine in the early afternoon, how could I have known? They look like tiny babies, Mamma. Little raw babies that died. You pick up a wing and the body comes after,

47

sprawling. Arms and legs dangling off. There is no head. I never met a man I didn't like. I never had a corpse without a head. Which, needless to say, called for two more bottles of Rioja fine Spanish wine. He found me talking to the radio. I sat in our bright filthy kitchen with the phone in my hand. My hand hung off the table. I was talking to the radio about my life and its embarrassments. I kept on saying "But" and they kept speaking of their fiscal persecutions. Could you really tear off mattress tags? What if a new car ran like something old? How do you tell your darling's baby-sitter that she has bad breath. I said to the phone "But what if she *likes* it bad?" I kept on saying "But." He put me to bed. I fell asleep apologizing. I woke in our bed and went downstairs. I walked around the house all night. Swallowing aspirin. Apologizing to the darkness. He was awake upstairs. I knew that. He was the darkness I kept saying "Sorry" to. He knew that too. In the cottage we lived in near Salisbury, England. The house was made of corrugated tin and shaped like a pail. The roof was shaped like a lid. Something not shaped like a hand all night was lifting the lid and slamming it on. No warning. Off. On. Slamming. Shaking us down like hard old garbage coming down. I came down in the darkness in my ski pajamas he bought me in Marks and Spencer's. I had his bathrobe on backward. The shoulders came under my chin and the sleeves went around me from the front. My sad plaid lover collapsing in on me. A strait jacket no one had tied. I sat on the steps that curved downstairs from our bedroom no one was using. I told him "It's just like they're shooting at us."

He was at the other end of the living room. All darkness, and he was looking out on the Plain. Standing by himself and watching explosions on the Salisbury Plain. He said "They aren't shelling anyone. They're having a practice. Night-firing, it's called. Tonight they're making believe."

"Well that's nice of them. I mean, not shooting at anybody. At least we have that to stay up with all night. That no one is dying tonight."

He said "Only of natural causes tonight. This is a very big night-firing exercise when everybody says things into radio-telephones like *I would like four quick rounds on co-ordinates Red Cross Charlie, please.* Everyone sounding like Horatio Hornblower. They're making believe they're at war. They're blowing little people up."

"As long as no one dies."

"Not from them they won't."

I said "When did it wake you up?"

He said "I didn't wake up. I didn't come to bed. I stayed here. But they only started a couple of hours ago."

"I didn't hear that. I mean it didn't wake me up. I was edging over in my sleep to get warm on you and I didn't feel anybody there and I got scared. So I got up." It slammed like tin. "It *still* feels like they're aiming at us."

Naturally he said "I'm sorry you had to wake up."

Naturally I said "I'm sorry you couldn't sleep."

And then of course he said "Why are we being so polite to each other?"

"Because they're shooting at us?"

"I told you they're *not*. They aren't, don't be dumb. Okay?"

"Of course. I meant it *felt* like they were. I meant it was spooking me. But of course I shouldn't be dumb."

He said "I'm sorry." Of course.

I said "Would you tell me what's wrong? Is there something wrong you could sort of talk to me about if you wanted to?"

"No."

So I sat on the steps at an angle of ninety degrees to him. In the room where the old lady always sat when she owned the place. When she was living. With no furnace and a thousand books. In her narrow chair in front of the enormous fireplace. Its wide oak mantle. Smoke pouring up into the room. Reading. Outlasting her sister and brother. Her trips through Europe. Filing all her sketches of Italian donkeys with her diaries upstairs where we found them in the leather trunk. Reading the

49

new books by Edith Sitwell and T. S. Eliot. And everything dark, the room and the plain except for its explosions with the cottage and the air around it every few minutes crunched. The way paper does when you squeeze it hard in your fist. When the guns didn't shoot the pigeons outside were grunting because they were scared. The drip of water off the heavy thatch. We stayed there and the guns went off and there was silence and the guns.

"I didn't mean to be vicious" he said.

"Is it the guns?"

"Partly them."

"Partly what else?"

He said "What if I have to go home?"

"If your father—"

"Does his famous dying act. Yes. Calls his life off and I have to go home."

"We thought about that."

"I thought about it more. It feels like he's dead."

"Oh no. Really? No."

"It feels like he's dead."

"I hope he isn't dead, Phil."

"So I get up in the mornings early or I hang around late and wait for the little red truck on Her Majesty's service to zip in here with the mail. Yes or no. I've been waiting this week."

"Well why didn't you *tell* me?"

"I sort of thought you knew."

"Well maybe I did."

"Why didn't you tell *me?* I can hear the bastard turn off the A30 when he comes before seven, which he sometimes does. Probably he can't sleep either. Before the trucks are on the road sometimes I can hear him. At the Pheasant, and at the farm with all the sheds full of hay. Shifting down at the first turn. Shifting up. Shifting down again for the second one, sharp left. Then the climb up in second and the left turn past the gravel mound and past the water tower—"

Wittily I said "Stop it. That's enough, that's enough. I hate it. Stop."

50

"But I *hear* that" he said. "Into third at the water tower and then I start to say *Slow down now. Let's get it over. Let's be done with it. Now you have to slow down.*"

"Please."

"I feel like throwing up when he doesn't. He ticktacks past the house on Her Majesty's wretched service."

"Please."

"I feel like throwing up right now just on principle."

"But why didn't you tell me? I mean I knew you weren't sleeping so well any more. But *this*."

He said what the hell he would always say. "I didn't want you to be worried. Since I'm this hero and everything. Then I guess it was the guns going on and off and I didn't want it all to myself any more. I'm sorry I told you."

"Of course. It's your function to suffer. That's why we got married. So you can suffer for me. That's why we came to England. So you could hurt more fully. So I would enjoy it more. Right?"

He didn't move at the window. He looked out to where you couldn't see anything. Stood still.

The guns went off and the house slammed. I said "Let's call home. Why not? Let's put the call through and let them say everything's fine."

He said nothing.

I said "Should we do that?"

He said nothing.

I said "Please?"

He said nothing.

I said "Please? Could you tell me *any*thing?"

His breath came out. Then he said "Don't worry" and we both began to laugh. He whinnied and clicked. I giggled into the bathrobe's back. Then he said "Oh Christ. Oh Jesus Christ."

I said "Won't it be all right, really? Don't you think?"

He said "I don't see how."

I said "Then we'll go home and do it."

"That's what we'll have to do."

I said "Don't you hope we won't? I hope we don't."

51

The guns went off. Concussions beat on us like oceans. He leaned his elbows on the window sill and looked at the black glass and the blackness outside it. I sat on the steps.

I said "Well it hasn't just been Stonehenge on the stunning historical Salisbury Plain in peaceful old England."

"Porton? Well. A little poison gas between allies."

"No, not poison gas. Bacterial antipersonnel agents. Biological research, you know."

He said "They don't say it very straight, do they? But how do you talk about all that dying straight?"

"Nerve gas, anthrax, polio. Did you know that? They keep *polio* bombs in there to blow up over cities if they ever need to keep the peace."

He said "It's scary. Everything's scary."

"And the helicopters. At night they look like bugs on fire. Blinking lights off and on."

He said "It's very scary." Then he said "Don't worry." Guns and our breathing, little movements we made. Then we sat very still. He said "Don't."

"Don't what?"

"I don't know."

The silence came again. The sound of the guns blew away. It came back. A window pane shimmied in another room.

He said "It's lightening up outside."

"The sunrise comes on the other side of the house."

"But it's still getting light a little. I can see the bushes across the road. There's something over there I can see."

I said "I have to go to sleep."

He said "It's time to get up, almost."

"No, I have to go to sleep. Don't wait for the mail truck" I said. "Come up. Come upstairs with me. Let's go to bed."

He said "I thought I'd wait a little while."

I said "No. Come up with me."

"It's light. I might as well stay."

I said "No. Come up with me and get under the covers.

52

We can sleep a little while with the curtains closed. You need the rest."

"Go ahead" he said.

"I have to go to sleep."

"Go ahead."

"I'll pull the curtains and pull the covers back and wait. I won't go to sleep until you're in bed."

He said to the window "Go ahead. I'll be there."

"I have to go to sleep" I said.

He said "I'm on my way now. You go on and I'll be there and we'll huddle in and sleep."

He stood at the window and looked. I sat on the steps under the arms of his robe. I said "I'll meet you." I closed my eyes and I sat there. He stayed where he was. We listened to the whine of the motor of the mail truck, turning off the highway, starting to climb.

For all I know, Mamma, that was your telephone call that died in the wires. Kicking in the hollow wires like a rat in an underground pipe. No law says you have to answer the phone. There's nothing you have to answer. *Yes* Nothing you have to come out of your mind to reach for and say "Come in." *Yes* I hate the goddam phone. I could wet my underwear I get so scared. I know—of what? I feel my heart start jamming into itself. My head hurts worse. I pick the phone up and the world comes pouring in. It makes a hole in me and the world comes in. My stomach beats. I'm hollow. My voice sounds wrong. I laugh when nothing's funny. Because I hope that no one will hurt me. I laugh to make them laugh. But: scared of *what?* Well I don't want to know. I know too much already. That's probably why my head hurts. If I could forget about half of what I know. Mix the other half with Spanish red wine, shake vigorously. Pour over a salad and eat myself. Brain-lobe dressing. It would probably give me headaches. That's why I didn't answer you, Mamma. Because it might have been you. Or Phil's mother dying. Or a sailor looking for a berth. I'm not responsible for people calling me. *Yes* So why do I keep writing

53

to you? In revenge for your stupid well-intended sadist letters? I keep trying to get home. Don't I. Trying to worm my way between your legs the way Daddy doesn't. Ramming up toward home. That's why in the middle of March I am writing you an endless letter that begins at nowhere no time and has no location or end. Undated. You and me, Mamma, we are a couple of undated chicks. And when I am dead you will survive me. To screw up the clocks. To prove that generations aren't made of young then old then young. To have a mother survive her child who survived her children. How does *that* clang the icy chain of generations? And you will be living and I will be dead. And you'll get hold of this that I never sent to you. You'll read it. You won't understand. You'll think it's something as simple as love and hate. Love and hate. When all the time you'll be reading my life. But you won't know that. Will you? But you'll be reading my life. And what if I end at Easter? What if I end on the first real clockwork day of spring? Will you have the splendid lack of imagination I've always counted on? To think I think I'm somehow Jesus Christ? That famous Jewish poet? Will you think I think I'm spring's fat goddess? Titless Mother Earth? Drooping belly and all. But I don't want to die. I want us to live forever in each other and not get old. We're getting old. A letter came for my fifteenth college reunion. The Massachusetts Colony Reunion Invites You Home! I wish I could go there like a ghost and watch them. It would be so sad. I wish I could see them and be invisible. Hang like a fog in the corner of the room. They would think I came from someone's cigarette. The pretty ones would be straining in their girdles. The boys who used to buy them beer and screw them in their secondhand cars would be tired. Lines of dresses strained around the stomach. Lines of strain tearing at the corners of their eyes. Drinking beer and not remembering when they said "Remember? Remember?" Or honestly recalling spring weather and how easy everything was. With no such thing as age. And ancient alumni ignored on party week ends. While they were standing still in time. Remembering that and

54

growing silent, then drunk, then weeping while everyone laughed and said "Good old—whoever you are." Whoever you were. Whoever I was. Or am. But I wish I could see them like a ghost. Am I a ghost to you, Mamma? When you read this when I'm dead will you think you're hearing a ghost? I wonder, then, if that's what I am. It feels like being alive. Dead is like being alive. It all depends on who hears you. Who's reading your life. *Yes* But I don't want to die. I want to get myself organized. I want to live in straight lines that end where they should. Like a poem. I want a little control in here. Pick the books up and put them away. Wash the dishes. Dry them, even. Drive to the village and do a wash. Clean laundry smelling hot and soapy. Lavender sachets in the bureau. Vacuum the closet. Wash the windows! Everything is smeary out when I look. I want to clean that up. Keep the windows open even if it's cold so that when he comes home the inside smells like the outside and there's no difference. Then we'll close the windows and start out new. Make it smell like us again. The way we want it to smell. A little control. Like a poem he would write if we could get a little order into the house. And fix the house up. Arrange the jacks downstairs so the floors don't slant. Finish plastering the bedroom. Make screens for the summer. Buy a book of seeds and order a gardenful of green and red that will sweat in sunlight. Blue crockery bowls of hot tomatoes from our garden. Yes. Clean the garden up when the snow melts. Drag off leaves and cut the brush we never got to. I'll do the cutting. Make the mower work and trim the grass. I'll do the trimming. Buy a clean pair of dungarees that hang on my ass like skin and walk in the village so he can see them looking at me. And buy him a new book of poems. By someone he never heard of. He used to read so much. He reads the Boston papers and whatever Baker sent us during the fall. Books about history. Baker wrote one. A book about the revolutionary war. A journal with something in it on frontiers. He looks at those, I don't know why. He never mentions Baker's name. Neither do I. I wanted to say I want us to live together well again and not die. We never mention Baker. As if he were dead. We never mention Baker and me. In his car like a college girl. He came all over my legs. Twisting away in the darkness parked near the barn. Crying. He was crying like a college girl. I walked to the house and came up here. On the extra bed. I put the pillow over my head with my hands. Someone else's hands wanting to smother me. They felt like someone else's hands, they pushed so hard. I gagged and cried only out. Never on the in-breath, only breathing out. I cried it all out on the mattress under the hands of whoever she was, trying to kill me. All night I breathed my own tastes under the pillow pushing me down. I wonder if Baker needed me or plain cunt. I didn't care. I didn't wonder. But it was nothing. Moving like that. Like riding a bicycle. Nothing. I wasn't there. My body stopped. That's when he tore out, crying. That's when I came in. My hands on the pillow, pushing down. Baker drove away. Phil put his suitcase in the barn that night after work. We didn't talk about him. A friend who died. His letter came and I threw it away. Phil knew I threw it away. He knows. He put the suitcase in the barn because that's what you do when you throw away a thing without committing yourself to throwing it away. It goes in storage. Like me. Him. Our quiet family. We're stored. Is that what you'll do when I die and you read this, Mamma? Will you throw me away? Can you throw a history away? Is that what you do with dirty torn time? *We are saying to you* But I don't want to die. Suicide sounds like medicine. Something you clean clogged drains with. I don't want to die. Those hands did, pushing the pillow down. You can't choke your body to death. I don't want to die. But there is so much death in me. I have to get a hold on myself. Yes. I need to hold on. I need to *grab* me. Tell myself things I should do. Do what I tell me to. I have to hold myself here. I need to make me an orderly life. Phil. He has to hold me with his broken hand. He has to come at night and pull the pillow away from my head and tell me to breathe the way he says. Because I can't keep myself in line. Like a poem. I can't make my life work right. I need him to tell me.

Like a child. He has to hold me like a father holding a child.
When his father died Phil closed his lips tight. You couldn't
have gotten a finger in. Not the edge of a sheet of paper. Not
the point of a pen. Nothing. His face was dirty looking, he
went so pale. Something like the color of a stone. He sat in the
chair near the fireplace in the cold dark English living room
she used to sit in reading before she died and her niece became
our landlady, renting out a hundred years of her dead aunt's
wasting past. The little red mail truck came at seven-thirty in
the morning. There was still frozen fog in the garden. Dark sky,
stony as his face. All the trees and bushes bright white. The
grass bright white. Everything quiet, then the birds beginning,
then seeing him not there. Lying still while things warmed up.
Standing still at the bedroom window looking at the garden.
Downstairs he was standing at the roadside window looking out.
The sound of the mail truck's gears. The brakes stopping.
Footsteps so loud the ground outside sounded hollow. So I knew
it when I heard the footsteps and came downstairs to hold him.
I was crying. He was in the chair. His lips were so tight the
only air came in and out his nose. He was dirty-colored white.
The living room was cold. I said "Yes?"

He nodded his head and looked away from me.

I said "Don't run too far from me."

He nodded his head.

"Don't run too far."

He said this in a terrible voice. He sounded like a boy
being brave. He said "They couldn't call me up."

"Well, honey, there was nothing you could do—"

"They said he took a week to go. In some hospital in New
York. So why couldn't they call me up?"

"Maybe they were scared. Maybe they didn't know what
to say to you?"

"I could of seen him."

"Oh Phil. I wish I could hug you."

"Yeah, well don't do that now. Okay?"

"Okay."

"I wish they had called me."

"Would you have known what to do?"

He went so small and helpless. Like an old lady a hundred years before. His shoulders bounced and he made them stop. His face shook. He made it stop. He said "No." He said "I wouldn't of known."

I stayed where I was. My face was tight as his fists.

He looked at me. So much darkness behind his eyes. The world outside all white and frozen. He said "I'm so damn *mad*." He broke like the ice knocked off a tree. Shattered into what I held. Both on our knees in front of the old lady's chair. Crying and crying. Little babies in the world. The suck of air along the floor the chimney pulled out past us. Everything cold. We shook together. We came home. We flew into New York City and landed like immigrants. Pilgrims. Too scared to look at each other all the way through customs. Criminals. I thought they would put us in jail. But we waited for that. Mamma, how will he do it when Daddy dies? And will you be alone when I'm dead and you are reading this? Will you show it to Phil? Should I write something here for Phil to read? I wonder what to tell him that he doesn't know. How about Phil I Love You. Phil I Love You. Phil if you don't know that then what are you doing here with me in hell? But I don't want to die. Butcher, baker, candlestick maker. I don't want to be dead. Like that old lady all alone in her thatched-roof house in Wiltshire County, England. Smoke coming up from her fireplace. All alone with her books. Making watercolors of what she saw in Italy when she was young and there were possibilities. There are possibilities. Late at night in England we were both in bed. I was sleeping. I saw gentle sweet-smelling smoke come into the room. All white. It hung between the ceiling and the bed. Just hung. Because it belonged there. That was what I knew. It scared me. I closed my eyes in my sleep. Though my eyes were already closed. I closed them more. Then I said *Open your eyes*. Or the smoke said. Or I said. Or the smoke. *Open your eyes*. Then I said or the smoke *If you want to know her open your eyes.* In my sleep I opened my eyes. Though my eyes were closed with sleeping. They were also open. I saw the whiteness of something she wore when she lived in the house and slept in the bed we were sleeping in. She said *Is this what you want?* Or I said. Or the smoke. *Is this what you want? Is this what you want to know? Backward and forward. Or stay. There's time to decide.* In the morning I said "Phil, I want to go to Italy."

He said "If there's money left."

"No, I really want to go."

He said "Okay. Okay. Let's see how the money holds out, there's plenty of time to decide."

Then he started spending nights at the window. And his father died. We came home. But still. There is time to decide. Yesterday was the fifteenth day of March. Five days and it's spring. Last night it didn't snow. It was gray outside this morning. Things were dripping. Ice breaking up beneath its weight. The roads are black. The sides of hills show through. There's a sound of motors in the afternoons. Tractors spreading manure on the snow to melt in. People are planning for corn to grow. People are counting on crops. What if we decide to try once more? Is that the membrane stretched between us? If I'm not old-fashioned crazy and it's simple as that. If there's something really more, is that the membrane in our lives? Stretched between us like a chain. The maidenhead between Sorenson and his newly virginal whore. What if that's the membrane in our lives? And he is the prick and I am the cunt and what we're doing is sneaking up to the world's first fuck. Everything we lost sealed away somewhere. Everything we did forgotten. Starting not again but *first.* Waiting for the first time. Starting our lives. Starting a life. Spreading cowshit on the snow and waiting for the melting to be done. Sinking fertilizer in. Spring planting. First planting of the year. Of our lives. Everything buried away. This letter stopping, Mamma. Never writing you again. The ink put away, the paper, the pen. Burning Baker's book and his historical journals. Closing this room off. Reading novels. Writing poems. Making a book of sketches and then painting again.

His father not dead. Just not here. Unmentioned. Daddy and you someplace away. Not writing to you. No more writing like this. Not dying. Not England. No such place as Italy in the world. Saying "Okay. It's time to begin." Beginning. Tearing the membrane open. Something like pain. Something like a little blood. Except. Yes. Except what could we put on his hand that would look like a finger? What could he wear so we couldn't see it wasn't there? What can you hold without a thumb? We'll have to work on that. *You may not choose to leave us you must bear us in the world you are swollen with us Mamma* Mamma, I don't want to die. What can you hold without a thumb? *The wind that sucks along a cold floor* She said or I said or the smoke *There's time to decide.* Isn't there? *Yes always every minute you must* So I have to decide, I think. Is there plenty of time? Or do I have to decide about it? *Yes* His poor terrible hand. He writes with his left hand now. He's learning to write with his left hand. Like a child in school. The letters are round, then jagged. They slant down to the low right side of the page. They fall. The strokes are high and shaky. Then they fall. Like something written in a mirror. A kid on his first day in school. He left me a message at the table in the kitchen. It said *Hey have a good day!* Except at first it looked like *Help & good dog!* Like something in a mirror. We look at each other from mirrors. I wonder if he sees me flat and skinny as a boy. Shall I ask him to write you a note, Mamma? You could clip him something from the papers on the use of artificial limbs. If he writes his poems again he'll have to do it on a typewriter. I have heard of a poet working with a machine. Except that's what he does every day. He drives a machine. If he uses a typewriter will he drive it, I wonder. Or will the keys strike him. Maybe he'll write with his left hand. Poems in a mirror. By a little boy who's learning to write. *Help & good dog!* If he writes them. What if he doesn't? What if we don't try? Plant nothing. Make our spring another fall. Grow brown leaves. Dead thistle. Keep the membrane stretched. Stay who we are. A thumbless poet who doesn't

60

write. A virgin childless mother whore. I don't want us to die. If we live like this the rest of our lives will we be dead? I saw a crow drop past the window with a crawly thing in its mouth. Feathers at the edges turning up, adjusting. Glide, glide. I would like to sail without flying in the air. No beating wings. No effort. Sailing, gliding, moving smooth. But with nothing in my mouth. Nothing on my back. Just me, falling forward like a heavy bird. Going on. Or Phil and me in a heavy smooth car, a new one. Everything dies in the old one. Seatbelts on and drinking beer from a sixpack balanced on the hump between us on the floor in the front. Driving to Maine in this heavy car. Swaying, sort of ambling on. Going to the sea. The Harpswells. Driving on the coast where all the signs say NAVY KEEP OUT and ARMY KEEP OUT. We would stop and put up stakes with cardboard on top near the end of the weeds by the sea where you're not supposed to go. We would use our felt-tipped pens and write US—KEEP OUT and leave our message there and drive away. Buy more beer in a little store that sold pop instead of Coke and the only new thing would be Kodak film for the tourists. It would smell like wood inside, and raw meat, cheese, old cloth. US—KEEP OUT. We would drive into the army's sacred woods again to get to the sea. Drinking beer. Shivering in our raincoats until he got some ponchos from the car and covered us with them. Even our heads. We would be our own lean-to. Drinking cold beer and shivering. Leaning in on each other. Watching the ocean come in. Gray except where the waves broke. Gray as the sky. The same as the sky all the way out to where they joined. The sky and ocean separating for us as they came to our shore. Sky or ocean, both, beating in front of us. The whole world gray as ancient ice. Beating in front of us. And breaking. Not coming all the way to land on us. Beating in and in from all the way left and all the way right and all the way out. Coming in and coming in from everyplace. And breaking in front of us, white and foamy, nothing but bubbles of air and waterdrops. The longest heaviest sound in the whole world coming in at us but always leaving us alone.

Us safe underneath our lean-to. Leaning together and watching the entire world come in. Me falling with my face into his arm or chest or shoulder and crying and crying and never stopping and crying and crying back at the ocean and not stopping and still being safe, neither of us saying any words. Crying it all back at the ocean until it would be stupid to cry any more. Then turning our backs on all of it and driving past wire and signs and machinery buried in bushes to the little road past the two summer cottages empty because no one in New York or Boston was freed yet to get to the world. Past the boats dragged up into basins of cracked mud while the tide was out. The kelp and bones and shells all over the yellow sand. The little wooden houses where the people lived all year. The curve of the basin into the beach where you could stand and look across the water and see the little village climbing a hill and turn around and see the stores and doors where people lived. And sticking out over the water on black and brown piles draped with stuff that grows from the sea the old man's tiny store. Nothing inside but his fat dog that didn't move. Just groaned like a person. And the pictures on the walls of girls with the hugest tits and giant nipples, fat thighs spread apart. The giantest snatches in New England talking to the tourists from New York. But only us and the old man now. Picking out our lobster and driving back to the farthest sandy part of the cove. In sight of houses and stores, but all by ourselves. With the Coleman stove on the tailgate, a pot filled with seaweed and water boiling. Crushing the lobster into the pot. Breaking it to stuff it into the small black pot. With Phil not looking because he never could look at that part. Me saying "But you can eat em, can't you? So why can't you kill em?" like an old New England wife. But not being that. And making bad black overboiled coffee on the other burner and then us under our ponchos on a wet black log at the end of the beach. Watching the gray broken water beating. The beating of the sky. Eating our lunch and burning our mouths. Not saying any words. Then driving back to the US NAVY KEEP OUT reserve and driving off the road. Him making a shelter out of our ponchos with string and sticks for us. How would he do that without his thumb? Would I have to help him? Would he let me? Would he stay all silent and grim, fumbling? Would I start to talk about his hand? If I know me. You bet a life or two. I would tell him something and drive it all away. Or he would get it set and roll out bedding and we would talk about a nap and grin and get in under the canvas, looking up. And it *would* be lighter inside than out. Of course. And then I would say something like Boy, it's just like being in England—being on a military preserve and all. Something like that. And the words would drive it all away. They would carry the day away. Wriggling. Like that hanging-down thing in the crow's mouth. And what would we say, driving home in the dark? While the afternoon was carried away like a worm. Yes it's definitely melting into spring. I see straw-colored grass near the black trees. I see water pools in some meadow places. I can hear cows on the wind which means the farmers are bringing them out because it's nearly the spring. The black trees and gray trees are heavy with birds. Singing fruit. The branches are shaking with feathers. Do you think I would like carrying worms back home in my mouth, Mamma? With a tiny scrunched-up face here waiting in the crib you bought for us four years ago and the tiny smells of vomit and whatever else you smell when a baby is living in your house. His eyes always closed. His fists clenched tight. Little face laid flat on the sheet. Bald head. The sound of his sleeping. Phil would always be coming in to see if he was breathing. He is always checking to hear that I am, too. I hear him sometimes when I sleep up here. Outside on the wooden floor of the landing. Creaking, then standing still. I never know if he's coming into me and stopping, or standing there then going away. Poised. We're poised. The season is poised. Living is poised. This is where we wait. A family in waiting. Confinement. Twice. America twice. We started babies twice. Twice they ended. Twice we started again. Twice we weathered seasons and the year began. Symmetries, sets, arrangements, Mamma! What a

63

fucked-up fucking joke this joke is. Just, I didn't know they made the craziness so *neat*. Like nightmares into dreams. Dreams like living in a real life. Twice. Life like something you could bear. *Twice* There was something in the local papers last night. The usual rules against communism and pleasure and then a thing on a sea otter some Frenchman deep-sea diver naturalist trained. He was afraid of people but this diver trained him anyway. The diver named him *Esprit*. He learned to come to the diver to get fed sea urchins. Then the diver went away. An abalone fisherman came hunting. They hate otters. They eat the fishermen's income. So he called this little otter over and it came, which otters don't usually do. Then he shot a shotgun into him. Then he died. Which means don't think the world owes you an urchin. It could mean maybe you should change your name. Or anything else. That's the luck in being a painterly type. You get such colorful ambiguities out of nothing at all. What just occurred to me, Mamma—what if I do die and you do read this. What if we all do our job and you start out reading this and you turn out not to be what I think? I'm saying I expect some weeping here, Mamma. Some mournful noise. Some obligation toward your girl. Some discharge. Of obligation, needless to say. Some old-fashioned, say, nineteenth-century emotion. Tears and swooning. Because I have the feeling I'm not to be trusted. I have the feeling there's some motive in this. All this endless letter-writing. All this raving into my ear. I'm wondering how much I enjoy all this, Mamma. Plenty, I believe. I don't think I'd stop if ever my life felt good. So what I wonder is, what if you deny me? What if I die and you read this and halfway through you say to your color television set, your plastic wall-hangings, the sets of matched dinnerware and stemware and underwear "What a tub of drivel, ladies and gents. And now a commercial." *Click!* On comes a cartoon of a tall girl with no tits and her forearms too long. A little too hairy about the nape and upper lip. Two coffins drop from her skinny thighs. They fall feet first into the ground and root. We hear them root. Like beetles eating leaves if you're quiet. The coffins grow until they're lady-size. Zoom in on coffins. We hear the tap of little fingers scratching. The coffins crack like shells. You know what comes out? Twin darling girls! Each one looks like me! The same full size! The exact same paranoid face! Same thighs! They spread! Two coffins fall from each. The coffins root! They hatch! The twins of me leap out! They spread and drop and then the coffins hatch! I'm born again! The pictures move faster! Too fast to see! Soundtrack full of laughter! Coffins, daughters, laugh! Blackout, and back to you. Reading this. You put it on a coffee table. Later you put a cup of coffee on it. Then a plate with half a pineapple-cheese danish. Ash tray, cigarettes and lighter. Part of a swell timely dress you're sewing. Newspaper. In the afternoon, exactly at four-thirty, a light Scotch-and-water. Next day a coffee cup, fresh cigarettes. A half-eaten crab salad sandwich. Invitations to something to be addressed. Invitations to answer. A note that says *Write to Phil.* A bill for burying me which you can finally face. A letter from Phil wondering why you snatched the body to bury. Another note: *Write to Phil.* Letter from Phil demanding my body back. Letter from Daddy. Who had to fly on business. And you, saying "I have *got* to get this room cleaned up." And under everything, me. Saying this. So silent. Well. No law you have to listen, Mamma. So I wonder why I'm saying this. Anything. Because I can't even remember what I started to say. The radio says the deer are moving out of the forest into the fields. People in their cars are watching them. The deer are watching back. Everyone's afraid the deer will pull their rifles out. Start shooting innocent bystanders. Don't you wish they would? Because I wonder if there *are* any innocent bystanders. Just in case you wanted to know. So what if you don't read this? What if you read it and then don't care? Two different problems. If you don't read it maybe I'll still be alive. I don't want to die. If I do. If I do. If I do and you read it and then don't care. Maybe that will mean I'm *really* dead. Maybe that's when you're good and sure-as-shooting dead. When nobody hears what you say. So what am

I doing here, Mamma? Staying alive? *Is this what you want?* she said. Or the smoke. *There's time to decide. We are your clock* But if you don't read this then am I still alive? I wonder if now I am living. *We are your time* All night it's rained. Until I forgot I heard the rain come down. And then I forgot I was listening. Snow. I didn't hear the weather harden. But this morning it's snow. The trees hard white. Ground is white. The birds are still in the trees, shrieking. The trees bounce. The birds go on. The sky bright gray, light enough to make your eyes hurt. Don't look. Thank you. And the twenty-third of March. No wonder he left early, banging the door. I thought he was angry at me. He was mad at the snow. The world. Why not? I thought he was angry at me. I wonder why I do this so much in the mornings. I should write you at night, Mamma. At night I'm too tired, though. From doing nothing at all. It makes you tireder than anything else. I have to sleep so much. I'd sleep more if the headaches went away. Try sticking aspirin under your fingernails and sucking the tips until the pain disappears. Fast-acting fingers for faster relief. Yes. Don't I know it. Having tried some finger-fucking in the recent past. Yes. Well you have to live. Yes. Don't you. Why? I wonder who's talking on this page to me. Because I am not about to start an Albert Camus discussion. Look what it got him. He drove into a tree. Shmuck. Even a novelist should be able to tell the difference between a tree and the rest of the world. Question time again, children. Who do you know who is happy? Whom do you know whom is happy? Delete. Delete. Who's happy. Thank you. Everyone I ever knew who left. Repeat. You heard, you heard. Everyone who is no longer in my life. Baker too, I bet. He couldn't deal with knowing me. And Philip Sorenson the famous non-Jewish poet. Fingerless Phil. Writing like a kid before a mirror. Learning to write, like a kid. I wonder what our life is really like. I mean if someone had a camera going on us. Nothing to filter out what really happens. Not how I see it. Not how he sees it. Though *that* is something to know, I bet. Poor bastard husband victim Phil. But what really goes on? How self-conscious am I really? How much of this shit is phony shit? What do I say that's real? And what do we *look* like? What will you think I was, Mamma? When I'm dead and you are reading this. Or stopping in the middle, saying "You should have got laid, dumb daughter. Me and you. Scratch in the snatch and back in business." Right? Who will you think I have been? Like the time in England we drove the car to Bath. And the needle kept saying it was too hot and Phil still got mixed up. Driving every now and then on the wrong (right) side of the road. We found out it was the thermostat. Car getting hot. Like me. And it kept on boiling and everytime we would pull off under the trees and look at farms where people lived. Unlike this old farmhouse. And then going on. Green farms and green fields and the trees so old they were green with moss. Then going into Bath on Sunday and getting lost. The whole city quiet. Except for the kids who chased each other in and out of those buildings. Those old buildings. All that time. Those little boys running in and out, looking for something to steal. And somebody's sister who couldn't keep up. Dressed like a boy. Crying. Crying. And then that old restaurant where we drank the water that tasted like poison which everyone drank to stay healthy. Which was doubtless a moral lesson for us all. And down into the baths. The red and gold and clay all over. Tones I would give. Tones I wanted to make. Then, I really wanted to *get* them. Like those kids, stealing. I wanted the colors. The color of all of that heat. The huge quiet bath like a swimming pool with old gray steps where the king would bathe. Our noises being lost in the wet heat. And then looking up and seeing there wasn't a roof. It was the sky over us. And on the rim of the opening where the sky tried coming in there were those statues. The size of men. The guards with their swords and their spears. Looking at us. Keeping us in. Or keeping out the world. And into the chamber where they dug up the bones and put them in a glass case. A man and a woman. Little skeletons, they looked like kids. Just bones with petrified rags on. And the woman had no hands. The sign said they chopped off the hands of adulterous women or thieves. So why did Phil lose a finger, Mamma? When I should have lost my hands. And next to the case, a wooden door. I opened it and went in and the hole went down to the bottom of the world. I gasped because I was scared. Then I choked. Because the steam came up so hard it blinded me. I was lost in the hot steam. Crying. Crying. Like a little girl who couldn't keep up. And Phil came in and pulled me out. Like the church in Sherbourne. The city all amber colored. Another tone I wanted to keep. Which I never put down. The quiet church. The glass plate set in the floor which lit up when he stepped on the button. We looked down and saw the warrior from a thousand years before. All bones and rags. I screamed in the church and a man came running out. I said "I'm sorry. I'm sorry. I thought it was someone I knew." He didn't laugh. He showed us where Thomas Wyatt was buried. He told us Wyatt was the father of the sonnet. He showed us where a poem by Alexander Pope was carved on a wall. A really lousy poem. Phil kept going back to the little stone in the floor with Wyatt's name on it. He kept looking at that. I kept going back to the glass on the floor. I was frightened of stepping on the button to get light. I walked around and around, looking down. I didn't turn on the light. I looked down at the dark glass and saw myself reflected. Dead for a thousand years. Phil told me I was dumb. I told him he was dumb. He stayed where he was, looking down. And I looked down where I was. We stayed like that. I said "Phil, come here."

"Wait a minute."

"No. Come here. Please."

"Just a minute, I'll be right there."

"Phil?"

"Honey—*what?*"

"Would you please not let me get old?"

He stood up and looked at me. I looked away. At the dark glass. He said "You won't get old. You've got time."

I looked at the glass. I said "Says you, buddy."

He said "Who else should know?"

"Yeah. Says you."

68

And we came home to New York and America and here. For dying people. For us. Dying. There is time to decide. Yes. And now he knows. I'm his clock. And what I wonder, Mamma, is how long he'll stick it out. Ha ha. Not very far. Ha. But I really wonder. How long? And now he's driving a goddam snow plow through these little slippery roads because spring never comes where we live. And not writing poems. Not showing me any. What if a camera was going on us? Would it show him at his old desk in the little shed behind the kitchen? Doing secret poems with a handwriting like a kid? Like words in a mirror writing? Code? And almost time for the ducks to lay. He'll set the eggs in that little cabin he runs. And keep the heat right. Watch them hatch. He'll be their mother. Here comes the car with the mail. Yesterday Phil came home from work in time to bring the mail inside. Sitting here, watching him drive away and then come back. Nothing happening in between to pass any time. I didn't write a word to you, Mamma. I sat here. Waiting for anything. Then Phil came back in the state's pickup truck, bright yellow light on top. He parked in front of the house, below me. Walked across the road to the mailbox and then back inside, below me, out of sight. Walked the way he used to walk before everything happened. Or before I stopped helping him out with our life. Up on his toes, sort of bouncy. I heard floorboards squeak downstairs in the kitchen. Then on the two-level staircase. Up outside this door. Then his breathing. The wait. Then his knocking on the door. "Hey Honey? Babe?"

Through the door: "Hi Phil. Everything okay?"

"I came home."

"Everything okay?"

"Yeah. Yeah. I just decided to come home."

"Can you *do* that?"

"I did that."

"But I mean *can* you."

"Here I am."

"Shmuck."

"Listen, babe—"

"Phil, do you need me out there right now?"

"Why?"

"Well, I'm kind of busy in here. Kind of working, now."

"You're working? You're making pictures in there?"

"No."

"What kind of working?"

"Phil—I'm *in* here. That's all. I'm in here. I need to be in here for a while. Okay?"

"No."

"Phil—"

"No. Open the door."

"Listen, Phil."

"Open the door, babe."

"Later. Phil? I need—"

"Shit. Open the door."

"Phil—"

"All right. Now open the fucking door."

"Why can't I be alone?"

"You can be. You are. All the time."

"Well I'm sorry."

He said "I know you are. I swear it, all right? I really do swear that I know you are. That you are truly sorry for what—I don't know: whatever it is. We are. I know it. All right? But now you have to open the door."

"I don't want to come out, Phil."

"You don't have to. I want to come in."

"No!"

"So open the door now, babe."

"Oh *please*—"

"Because I'll play cops-and-robbers. Right? You know that. Right? You know how much I love to play that stuff. I'll put my fucking foot through the fucking door and walk right in full of splinters."

"Stop saying fucking so much."

"Oh."

"Well you don't need to say it all the time."

70

"I'm not saying it all the time. I'm saying it now. What? Two or three times. Does it offend you?"

"Phil—"

"Because if it does, you should try the real thing. You'll lose your fears of fucking."

"Oh."

"Don't give me oh. I'm not here for a coffee-break rape. I can get my ass someplace else. Just open the door. Now, babe. Right now open the door."

"Someplace else?"

"Now!"

"It isn't locked. Why did you think it was?"

"What?"

"I said it isn't locked."

Nobody said anything. Then he said "I wonder why I thought it was locked."

"Or why I didn't think I needed to lock it."

"Or that."

I said "Or that."

"What the hell is *that* supposed to mean?"

"You know, I have absolutely no idea."

"That's my girl. Whoops—"

"What? That I'm your girl? We're playing innuendoes now? Okay. We can do that. What else shall we nearly say?"

He said "I'm not playing anything. Except—"

"Open the door."

"What?"

"You're so hot to come in, Phil, then open the door. Come in."

And I actually closed my eyes. Put my head down on the little desk like a school child hiding. Clenched my eyes closed and shoved my forehead onto my arms on the desk. Waiting and waiting and then the door clicked closed. I was breathing fast. I heard him suck his breath in. Sounding as scared as I was. He said "Holy God."

I said through my arms "You never were in here before?"

"I guess not."

"You mean it's a mess?" Through my arms.

He said "Baby, you're the mess. It's a mess. You're the mess. Everything. God."

So of course I started to cry.

He said "Now."

I kept crying on my arms.

"Now. Now. We'll both get better. Everything—we'll be all right, babe."

"Sure. Listen. I happen to know I'm going mad. I sit up here and write this—"

"What?"

"Nothing."

"Okay."

"No—I stay up here. Or anyplace else around the house. I keep staying away from you. We don't talk. We don't screw. Nothing gets better. I don't even know if you're eating any meals."

He said "I'm fine. You never cooked so hot anyway and for God's sake forget about meals."

"Except I know you're a liar, Phil."

"So what else is new?"

"You'll tell me everything's okay and then go downstairs and shoot yourself because everything *isn't* okay."

He said "I won't shoot myself."

"Well. Something. You never tell me the truth if the news is bad."

"Yes. Yes. Except there isn't any *news*."

"What?"

"Nothing's new. Nothing's going on. It's all the way it was last summer. The way it's been all autumn long. All winter."

"Everything's the same."

"The same."

"Oh Phil. That's no damned good, is it?"

"It could be better."

"How?"

"Take your head off your arms. You don't have to open your eyes. There's nothing to see. You don't have to look at a thing. But move your head up so I can see you."

"Why?"

"Because that's what you should do."

"Why?"

"Because there aren't any more *whys*. Just what you do. After I ask you, what you do—that's the whole thing. Please."

So I kept my eyes closed and moved my head. It shook with the crying. I held it there.

He said "Thank you."

My neck hurt with the holding. I stayed that way. My body began to shake with staying that way. He put his heavy hands around my throat as if he was choking me. But he was holding my head so he could see. I leaned on his hands. The one without the thumb didn't hold. It lay there against me. When I opened my eyes his face was level with mine. He was kneeling next to my chair. His eyes were closed. His head was shaking and his face was wet from tears. I said "You're such a prick, Phil."

He said "Who else would stay with such a useless cunt except a useless prick like me?" He pushed my head down onto my arms. I moved it up, then opened my eyes. He was going out the door. He said "Okay" and closed it.

"Okay what?"

"Just okay. I don't know. Okay" he said from the other side.

"Phil?"

"Sure."

"Sure *what?*"

"What the captain of the *Mayflower* said to the Pilgrims —It may be full of monsters needing to eat us, but it's home."

"Ha ha."

"See you tonight."

"Ha ha."

"See you tonight."

"Tonight. I hope it doesn't snow any more. Phil?"

He was going down the stairs we've never fixed. I heard the wood groan. I heard the squeaks on the kitchen floor. The front door open and shut. The truck start up and go. The sound of nothing in the house but me. Needing to eat us. But it's home. Of course he left the mail, Mamma. Of course there was a letter from you. Daddy had an incident in New York. When a man's heart tries to stop they call it an incident. How neat. You wonder why he doesn't retire. Well because he'd have to stay home with you, Mamma. I don't know. If you read this far you'll think I'm trying to be mean. You ought to know. I don't have to try. It's like breathing. It's my natural skill. If you don't read this I won't have died. Maybe I'm still living. *Yes* Ovulating, I thought that's what it was. First the stab on the right side. A few days of that, every now and then, kind of sneaky. Bending down to pick up my mind or a falsie and feeling the little stab. Then the heat coming. I can feel it hot. The skin feels hot. The flesh inside feels hot. Like a boil inside in the tissue. I feel the edge pucker. I carry a wound. My outside should be swollen but it's not. But it should be. And the heat beating out. The edge inside on the heated tissue curling out. And not being able to move without making faces. Biting my lips like a heroine. Eating aspirin. Forgetting the headaches. And sitting still. Because I feel the edges pucker. When I look in the dark glass or the window with the lights off I am flat and plain and smooth. But I feel myself tearing inside. Like soft fat on the edge of a piece of pork. And the heat. I feel the egg pushing out, falling back. Pushing out of the torn tissue. Falling back. Then out and the pain is gone. A tender feeling inside like tissue remembering the pain. But the egg is out. I can move. The egg is in the Fallopian tube on its useless trip into blood. I wonder if I have cancer of the brain. These headaches. Which would explain why I can't get a little life like mine organized. Why I don't understand things. And don't take care of Phil. And want him taking care of me and don't let him. Hiding up here like

74

Emily Whatshername Dickerman Dickinson the titless recluse of New England and not coming out except at odd hours. Like when I am bound to be alone. All the time crying because Phil's not there. And thinking of Baker, the world's worst lay. And not even being sorry any more. For him or me or even Phil. Because what he and I did together for nine years, ten years, I wonder which. What Phil and I were. How could little Baker. Poor little Baker. Writing this letter to you, Mamma. Coming back into you in a pool of ink. Not wanting to tell what I tell. Wondering who *is* doing all this telling. Stacking all these pages up. Ticking away like a skinny motor. *Like a clock you are her clock we yours* Scattering all these words on all this paper all over this room I haven't seen since I've been here. You know what I would like? A long cold swim and come up here and find Phil sitting on the bed, the room swept up and all this shit thrown out. Me and Phil alone in this absolutely clean room. He would stand up and take all his clothes off. I would tell him he's grown a pot since he ran bare-ass last. I would hang a clean towel on his incredible erection. He would bounce on his toes to the door and pick up a hammer and ten long nails and seal the door. We would lie in bed together, rubbing. Screw or not. Whatever. The room would be cool. Nothing would hurt. I would say "Let's adopt a baby."

He would say "You really want to?"

I would say "I'm scared to. But maybe we should. Because once upon a time we didn't want kids because they would get in the way. Steal our privacy together away. But we don't have that."

"We don't have that" he would say.

I would ask "Could we get it?"

He would say "Let's get a new kind of privacy. With a fat little boy in it."

I would say "They wouldn't give us one. There aren't many kids any more. With abortion and all."

"Any *white* ones" he would say. "So let's get one that's

75

brown. If we like him, let's get another one that's yellow. Red. What the hell."

I would say "But what would happen to a brown baby?"

"He'd grow up" he would say.

"We'd die?"

"Well. Not right away. We'd get a little growing time too."

I would say "But I mean he'd grow up and we wouldn't be black—"

"Brown" he would say. Because he hates to think of people hating him.

"We wouldn't be black" I would say. "And he would not see us. We'd be dead. We'd die away from him. He'd tell us he was dead. We'd lose him. We would never see him again. No: I don't want to die like that. I don't want to—*do* all that and lose it."

"Him" he would say.

"Him."

I would lie on my back with my arms stretched out and my tits would disappear. I'd look at the dented gypsum board of the ceiling and the nails would fly out of the door like bullets and kill us. Which could all be from having a giant tumor pressing down on my brain. Giving me all these head-aches all the time. And making me so crazy. And anyway who says having kids is the answer? I don't want to have kids. I've *had* them. I've been milky-chested and waddling with people smiling at me on the street when I grunted along. According to *Woman's Day* those are the best times. Before they come out and act like people. Have a few years of their own time and leave you alone in yours. Yeah, *Woman's Day,* except I was always sick. And scared. And nearly dead a couple of times. Thank you very much. I've had my children. I've had my husband. All the people here have just about left. I'm almost a ghost town here. Like the movies on TV. Wind blowing through the doorways and boards banging. Mice running through the windows. All kinds of creatures around except people. They're all nearly gone. A ghost town collects dust and dead leaves and spiders do their work all over. A monument after a while. And the ghosts of everyone who died come back. All the times the ghosts once had come back. Everything happens in little white smoke clouds no one can see. Everything the ghosts ever did when they were people. All heaped up with leaves and dust and cobwebs. Old ladies reading. Young ladies writing. Husbands sitting up at night looking straight ahead. Snow falling after dark and disappearing in the daytime. Voices saying words no one's there to hear. Everything falling at night and disappearing in the day. Parents having words from their children and not quite hearing them. Everyone hurting everyone else. No one wanting to hurt. Everyone hurting. Ink all over the floors and walls like blood where a horrible murder was done. And no one finding the corpse. And dead fingers in the grass, growing. Rooting and growing up in the spring through corn snow and mud into sunlight. Moving around at night. In the daytime being still and pulpy and swollen like dying flesh. But not dead. Growing. Mamma, I don't want to be a ghost. I don't want to be dead. I want Phil to know that I'll be all right. I just need some time. For what? For what? She said or the smoke *There's time to decide.* But maybe she meant I have to decide about time. Which I don't understand. Maybe that's what she meant, though. Not that I had enough time. That I had to make up my mind about it. But what? What should I decide? I can't decide anything. My mind keeps moving. I can't get organized. What do I have to decide? But maybe that's what she meant. Because then he started staying at the window. And the letter came in the little red truck. And his father died and we had to go to his death. We had to go back to his dead body. To the end. And start there. Coming home to America and starting. We started a baby and he died. We came here in the woods and made a clearing and fixed our house. We made a fort and something got in anyway and the baby we started again died. The starting stopped again. But I don't know

77

where else we should go. I don't know what we should do. Because I'm afraid. Did she mean I had to decide again? To start again? Well supposing I decide I don't believe in ghosts? Stonehenge is just big rocks. Salisbury Cathedral is a church a bunch of bishops built. To put their dead knights' bodies into. Old Sarum Cathedral is a ruins. And England was a trip we came home from. That old lady stopped reading and died. Phil's father died. We came back to a place and my body lost some tissue we thought might take and grow and it didn't. What if that's what I decide? Is that a mind made up? How about that for deciding, old lady on the Salisbury Plain? Then why am I writing this, Mamma? Why am I saying this to you? Whatever it is. Whatever I am. Warehouse for cancer. Dead babies. Formerly occupied by husband with poetry and thumbs. He might occupy again, though. He might come back inside. Though I don't know why he should want to. But he does want to. Which is why we're together. Isn't it why I'm writing this, Mamma? It's the same reason he lives here. With no peace, nothing fresh or clean. Everything's a battle, but he lives here. Like some old Vietnamese man in a tiny little hut made out of tin and used-up cannon shells. Living with his skinny body and wrinkles and his muscles in his legs that always hurt. And the little skinny boy with him who was his daughter's son before his daughter got raped and killed by the Northern guerrillas and her husband was shot by the Southern police for letting his wife collaborate. And they live on nothing. Their stomachs hurt when they eat. The boy never cries. The old man touches him on the front of his bony throat when he sleeps, which he doesn't do too much of. In his sleep when the old man touches him the boy begins to cry and then wakes up. So they leave each other alone. They are living out of habit. They are living because they have to. They are living because they're afraid that they should. The old man lives because the boy does. Because he is a Catholic and the priests have told him about hell, the devils with Oriental eyes and bayonets not so different from what the

Japanese brought in 1943. The boy lives because he still is convinced that it is other people who die. He is who he is because he lives. The old man knows who *he* is because they will kill him next, or next after that. When they wake they hide from the guns and look for food. They sleep while the rocket-bearers and cannon spotters have their meals. Or at night because there is no food they sleep. In the morning he goes to plow snow. Or take care of brown baby ducks. Or build fences for the picnickers. Or help show a movie on conservation for a high-school science class. I wonder what he says to them. Any of them. The other men there who do what he does. I wonder if they know he's a poet. I wonder if he does. If they showed a movie of us now would it be a horror picture in the drive-in where people get laid while they're scared? So that later they can't remember the difference? If they showed us would we be a spook show? Or would they just show us the way we really are except show it in this underground cave where nobody watches except ghosts. *Yes* Would we be that scary if they ever told the truth about us? *Yes* And if they did show everything straight, the whole truth, nothing but blah blah, would he be someplace at night in our house writing poems? Because I would be so happy if he would. Even if he never told me. Why should he? What have I done for him lately? I've stayed here. Big deal. Typhoid Mary hung around too. I took care of his thumb. Yeah. And now the rest? The rest. There's so much other stuff to think about. Like why I write this to you. Why he stays here. Why I kill him. Why he isn't screwing girls in bars. Why I say he isn't. Why he doesn't aim the big plow straight west and go. Through mountains, knocking down trees. Cleaning out a forest to get west the hell away from me and my sweet forbidden fruit. Which is a dry snatch, a nasty disposition and a future so small I could stuff it in a cup of my bra. But what if we forgot it all? For about a day say we forgot about everything that happened in our past. Pull the plug on the kitchen clock, turn off the TV and radio and rip the an-

tenna off the car. Pull the blinds down and clean up the house
and drink sweet tea together and get some purified magical
holy grass and blow our brains out together until we feel like
jelly on a plate but full of hormones, jiggling. And screw for
twenty-four hours straight until we can't move. But not know
it's twenty-four hours. Not know the time. Forget a minute of
our history. And make a perfect spermy baby so oily in
come he's protected for every minute of his nine months.
And have him. Go the route. Throwing up and headaches
for a change and being scared all the time that I'll die. Swell
out like a sick cow. And Phil could nurse me back to health.
And we'd never talk about our history again. We would make
each other never say it again. Even when we got scared. Even
if we had huge fights. And we would just keep going. Looking
relaxed but being scared. Curled over and holding on and
going straight ahead the way he does when he drives the big
plow straight through snowbanks. Looking calm and tired.
Holding onto the wheel, bent over, going on. And have the
kid. And live. Not hurt too much. Maybe they could hypno-
tize me. From month four, on. Because I'm not as scared of
the hurt as I am of doing it again. Believing one more time
in my body. In the whole system that says bodies make life
come out. In the whole kind of world where they depend on
bodies making life not death. Believing it again and dropping
a little furry pile of bleeding pulp and little soft fingernails and
eyes sealed over with the softest skin. But not letting ourselves
talk about it. Living as if we invented the system. And going
ahead. Whistling a lot. And doing it. Pain and all. Having the
kid and sneering at the gooey nurses but crying when we're
alone. Calling him something like Mike or Spike. Or Billy. Ben.
And panicking and buying a hundred boxes of everything they
sell in the discount stores for kids. And two copies of Dr. Spock.
Rattles and teething rings and lotion and powder because I
always did think of the smell of the powder on his little
smooth back. Worrying about having enough milk. My tits
are so small. But they might. And if not they sell it in cans

80

and bottles. It's perfectly safe. They all use it for their kids. Their first and second and third and fourth. Their problem is to turn it off. My problem isn't. Why should I have to die for getting it out when they're working so hard to keep the eggs in? Life is definitely not fair. Which isn't funny. Because if it isn't, why have it? Why have something that doesn't work? Because, stupid. Because it works for itself. So why can't I be part of it? You are. You just don't like your share. This is stupid, Mamma. They pay football players good money to go to college and write things like this in their freshman year. So go be a boy. You look like one. Phil played basketball. He really believed in that. A crewcut. The team blazer. No screwing before the game. Steaks for breakfast. Now he gets old cold bacon fat for breakfast. Study hard all the time to keep your grades up and stay on the team. Live clean. He fucked the coach's wife or sister, daughter, something like that. He played it straight all the way through to his senior year. Then he just couldn't resist. Thank you coach for all you've done for my character, whump. So he never made it to the NI-something in New York. T. They left him behind. But the coach forgave him before they got on the bus. They lost by twenty points. Which goes to show you a definite moral lesson for us all. Butcher, baker, candlestick maker. I've made a candle or two in my time heh heh. But if he broke out that one time why couldn't he do it again. Or the times he's come up here and almost told me. Or asked me. Always he *lets* me. He lets me alone when I say I want him to. Or don't say it, and he knows it anyway. He lets me do all of *this*. But he's done it before and maybe again. Not letting me. Coming up here like he's climbing a mountain, he breathes so heavily sometimes. And almost saying something. But always staying quiet. Being strong. He stays so fucking strong I think about killing him sometimes. Because how could he be so strong if he didn't think he was right? And I'm wrong? Well maybe so. But maybe not, buddy. But maybe some time he'll come up here and not threaten. Just break things the way I've

81

seen him do it in our life and long times. Kick the door in. Go berserk. Scream at me until he shakes. Spit and sweat and drool. Step right through the bottom of a chair and kick it off his foot and out the goddam window! Saying "Okay. This is it. This is fucking *it!*" And tell me what to do. Say what I should remember and what I should forget and what I should learn how to do. The way he used to talk before we came here. Sell it all. It's not so much. Sell whatever we have and buy a new set of camping gear and fuel for the little stove and a new used car or a new car or fix the old pig we run. And take two knapsacks with some underwear and socks and old shirts in them and just go. The place doesn't matter. Except it has to be warm sometimes and wet sometimes and then sometimes cold enough to make you want to work whether you think you want to or not. Just go. And stay alone. Him telling me what. What not to. What. And staying alone together. Learning whatever we have to. What he says we have to do. And me staying quiet. Not obedient. No harem bullshit. No obedient wife bullshit with the straw still wet inside. But staying together. Learning. Maybe he has to learn too. Of course he does. His hand always in his pocket. Mamma, that's what we have to do. That's what we have to do again. Just like this except it didn't work this time or the place before in the time before. But that's what we have to do again if he tells me to. If he gets crazy enough and dizzy enough with the pain of living here with me like this and tells us what to do. Gets us organized like a wagon train and whips us out to wherever we can go, wherever he says we have to go, like tired oxen pulling a load behind us, whipped. And listen, this is what we call in the trade a red-letter day. Make no mistakes, Mamma. This is only the day the clock came around to. But it is the thirty-first of March, day preceding April First, April Fool's. At dawn on April Fool's Day I will sacrifice an Aztec to the sun. Also Good Friday, though. Which is what makes it so premeditated-seeming. Though it simply happens to be the day I'm writing this to you in case I die. Which I don't want to do. So listen, Mamma. Nothing intended here. Nothing cute. Just, this is the day it is. Do what you like with it. Kill yourself a Jew and nail him up for Christ. Chain your husband to a cross and force him out on the streets when the husbands are coming home from work. See how he handles being their parade. Stupid thing to write when I'm asking you for something. I wonder what I'm asking for. But I went out this morning after Phil went to work. So much snow was melting, I sank into mud to my anklebones. Across the road and up the little hill. Where the dead tree has arms and boles like a totem pole. It always looks like it was put there on purpose. Mountains and little hills in gray clouds and still with snow on them. A kind of greeny redness on the trees. Snow melting on the fields and birds in everything, screaming. Starlings and jays. I thought there was something wrong. It was only the way things always are in spring. And you're supposed to be so happy when it comes. Almost comes. I wore Phil's navy jacket and I still shook. But you're supposed to be happy. I was there smelling wet ground and I was scared. So I came back. Up here. Because does that mean I spend the rest of the year the way I spent the year waiting for the rest of it to come? Is this all there is? Because I can't live another season like this. I can't live in the spring like this. Like this in the summer. Into the fall and winter again like this. So listen, Mamma. I don't want to threaten you or anything. But the world had better change. *No* Or you won't have your sole surviving daughter as the sole surviving daughter any more. There it is, fans. You heard it here first. The daughter threatens her mother with her death. Change the time or I will beat the clock. But what if I die now? Mamma, if I die and you can push yourself this far, what will you think? That I really died because of you? Something keeps coming after me. Not you or Daddy. Though Christ knows you haunt me enough. And Phil? Phil. Not even Phil. All he does is lie on my conscience all the time like I'm a murderer. And Baker. No. Because he isn't Phil. But something. Like a sponge on the back of my neck I can't touch. All cold and slimy and full of weight. Like a snake. A little garden snake that lies on my cheek from my eye to my mouth and I can't touch it. Sort of like my headaches but not so much *there*. But there. Something ticking but there's nothing to tick. Which is why I said to Phil at dinner when he brought the pizzas home with a six-pack of beer "What would you say if I told you the house is haunted?"

He was leaning against the stove while the frozen pizzas broiled. Smoke from a thousand old hamburgers poured. He was squinting and waving in the air in front of him. The smoke kept coming into his eyes. Of course I wanted to cry for what I did to him. I always did to him. And always wanted to cry. He said "The one in England was haunted."

"Well?"

"Well what?"

"If you live in one haunted house is there a law says you shouldn't live in another?"

"I mean, you really think there's a ghost in here?"

"There's somebody here besides me."

"And me?"

"Fuck you, Phil. Stop taking me to task."

"Why?"

"Just stop."

"All right. I'm stopped."

"Please?"

"Yes. Yes. Yes. Is there something living here besides you and me and the usual rats and mice and spiders?"

"Yes. But I don't know about *living.*"

"You really mean ghosts?"

"Are you going to say it takes one to know one?"

"You think I should?"

"The pizzas are on fire."

"Do you think I should?"

"No."

"Then I won't."

84

"Why not? Phil—why wouldn't you say that?"

"You don't want me to."

"And?"

"You'd get a little scared."

"*I'd* get scared?"

"Because you think you are. I don't know."

"No, no. Hey, don't hide behind a flaming pizza, god-dammit. *I* think I am? I'm suspected of suspecting *I'm* a ghost?"

"Baby. I want to eat this plastic trash I bought. I want to drink some beer. I think you should too because you don't eat and you're getting too small and I don't want you to disappear. What I *don't* want to do is talk about if you are a ghost. You're here and I can see you and you're not a—for God's sake. For God's sake. Will you come *on?* Ghosts."

"Are you mad?"

"Hmh?"

"I said are you mad at me?"

"No."

"Why not?"

"What?"

"Phil!"

"Wow. No, I'm not mad. Yes I am. All right? Yes."

"Why?"

"Because I burned the goddam pizza on account of you. Because I burned my fucking *thumb* pulling it out of the oven. All right? Because now I have no thumbs to twiddle while I'm waiting for you."

"You're waiting for me."

"Listen." Melted cheese down his beard. Tomatoes like blood on his mouth. "What the Christ else would I be doing around here? You think I'm here for the annual long winter endurance contest?" He shook his head and the black and brown crumbs sprayed out. He put his hands down flat on the table. One with the thumb lifted up. Red right under where the nail should be that he'd chewed off. The other with a small puckered stump. Baby thumb. He closed his eyes and I went out. So when he opened them I was on the stairs. Hearing him shout "Oh listen. For once! Will you listen?"

Calling back "Well you can stop waiting, old friend. Don't let me detain you."

And the sound of things being thrown. Rage clanging up the stairs like someone behind me. Hearing "Son of a bitch goddam son of a bitch goddam *bitch!*" Okay, Mamma? And smiling. Darling daughter with her large famous smile. Because he was getting mad enough to tell me what to do. The question of course being whether he did. Whether he does. It's April the First. No, Mamma, that's what the calendar says. April One. I wish I knew the history of it. What someone did today a thousand years ago. In the morning the ice still freezes like skin on mud puddles. The dead curly grass is frozen. It looks like a hemp doormat. Then melts, defrosts. Like the lady who wanted to kill herself until she realized she hadn't defrosted the refrigerator for six months. And she was married to such an incompetent shmuck, she couldn't leave him alone to take care of *that*. So, so the story goes, she lived. All things being relative. She might still have died without the story knowing it. He might have died ten years before she thought about it herself. But pretty early on it all begins to melt. The ice skins turn to mud. You could walk through the grass and squish in water. All the birds are always in the trees. The sun looks different. Even when the sky looks gray in the morning it's a brighter gray. It swears it couldn't snow now. There's light all over everything, Mamma. Which could win me a merit badge for looking at things. Or not sleeping. Or being a little crazy. Or a lot. But what about feeling something else? When do I get glad? Or are you reading this and I'm dead and you're saying to yourself "That bitch daughter of mine would distort anything. Change anything true in the world around to something else. So she could make me sorry. Sad. Make me want to forgive her for never loving me enough. The wrong way, anyhow. For never giving me the babies you should give your mother. She gave you you. You could at least give back you again. A little different, but you. She could have you as a baby again. She could be you as the mother when she holds your child. Holding your child she could be you as she was when you were the baby. Holding your child she could be you as the mother. Holding you as the child she could be herself when you were the child she was holding. She could be everything she was. But you would not be the you you are. The you you are would be dead. But heavens I don't want anyone dead." Do you, Mamma? But would you believe what I've said. Are you reading this? Am I dead and do you believe me? Do you believe me? Or do you think everything is changed from what it was. And I wrote this while I lived to tell you things to make you sorry. Love me more. Forgive me. Forgive me. But you wouldn't say "you," would you? You'd say "I." Period next to the I. Right. So you'd say "I gave you you and give back you again if you're a good girl so I could hold you while I hold your baby and be you while I hold your baby and have the baby be you so I would be the mother and you as you now would be dead and you would be the baby and I would be the mother and no time would pass." Is how you would say it. But you wouldn't say that, would you? Do you? Are you now? Where are you standing or sitting or lying down while you read this? How did I die? Or am I dead now while I write this and don't have to die later to be dead while you read. Have I been dead a long time when you read this. And what if you don't read it? What if you throw it away. Saying "How about a few *facts,* daughter? What about telling the truth?" Throwing it away after reading a couple of crazy words. And I'm dead. Did I die twice by now? Three times? What happens and what happened. Either /or. Where *am* I if you stop reading this? How do you remember me? How will you remember me? How are you remembering me? If you don't know what this says. If what I say is true. Do I think it's true? Or am I changing things to make you love me more. Mourn me more. Be more sorry.

Be more forgiving. If I'm not changing things and what I say is true and you don't read this, how will you know who I am? Or if I change things not to hurt you. If I don't do this to make you forgive. If I say what I know. And if you don't read this. Then I'm dead. But if I don't give you babies and you don't hold them. Hold me. Be me. Be you when I wasn't me but only yours and tiny. Am I killing you? Do you hate me because you're dead? Because I killed you? Let you get old and changed? Didn't give birth to you, Mamma? By having kids for you? Did I kill you too? Are you dead because of me and I'm writing to a ghost? Am I dead when you read this? Am I dead because you never read what I'm saying here? Ghost talking to a ghost? Mamma? Is everything dead? Is anyone there? April Fool's. If I were big and strong. With heavy muscles in my legs and back. And knew where to go. If I were a man is what I'm saying. I would put a knapsack on my back and carry a fishing rod and walk away. To the Harpswells in Maine or someplace far away. Over the bridge in Maine to Canada. Walk to Alaska. Keep walking on big heavy legs. In old soft boots and woolen socks. With dehydrated food and a canteen and a first-aid kit and some warm clothes. A glove for taking food off the fire. And keep walking. Go away by myself into forests and little roads where cars don't go any more. And live by myself until I understand. If I were Phil. I wonder why he stays. Because of me. Of course. And all he gets is killed. I hope he doesn't. I wish he doesn't. Mamma, what do you do all day until Daddy comes home? What do you do when he doesn't come home? When he carries his heart to the office and lets it tremble there and doesn't come home? Always asking these questions and writing these words. In college we used to talk all the time but none of us could write. We would all be so proud of not being able to write. Painters as nonverbal. Images. We would always talk about images and how we didn't work in words. So here I am not painting. Or drawing. Or pulling prints. Or doodling on a scratch pad. Nothing but words. You can die of words. I

88

don't want to die. Mamma, I'm like you, I don't want to die, Mamma. *Mamma*

*S*o: *finally. Our father in the old parlor of their new house in Maine where they came in the summer in a rented truck and carried furniture and camp trunks and whisky boxes full of books through the slanting bleached doorway. He drove the truck back, our mother following in the station wagon, and they returned together (she still driving, smiling under her sunglasses) and they came on the one-lane road through the village, swinging right and onto a pocked rocky road, then right again, miles later, to a narrower dirt road, driving past low hills and blueberry bogs, down, past the white abandoned church on their right, the reaching empty fields across from it, down, until they turned off to an unpainted slanting house with a well in front, a gray falling barn behind it, the road continuing down through the jungle of fields around their house, down to the rocks and the sea, where it ended. And, at night, our father in the parlor, writing in his speckled compositions notebook with his left hand. The writing slants down to the right and falls. The stump of his right thumb dances as he writes. There are no electric lights, and he is lit by a greasy-chimneyed kerosene lamp, its wide wick throwing brown and yellow light, the color of old pages. Everything is mildewed, moist—the aqua-colored love seat, the low round Victorian table he sits at (carved with pine cones and mouthy bulges), the pink wing chair he leans from to write. Insects call in crescendos that die completely before the calls begin again. Our mother sleeps upstairs rolled in blankets on a naked stained striped mattress. Our father in his undershirt and khakis, unlaced boots, no socks, drinks from a can of warm beer, bends into the rot-colored light and writes in falling lines*

89

then stops. He drinks again, doesn't write, looks behind him at the dark silent sitting room, ahead at the darkened kitchen, its doorway that leads to the shed and, just before that, out, to the lawn, the boarded well, the narrow bony road that goes to the sea. That is how he sits. He sits in the light and writes to the darkness. Saying: What I must do is be simple and clear. I'm sure that narrative leads to sanity, and slowly, carefully, chiseling the details, I must make what's happening come from what's happened; that will tell me what's to come. I have to organize, pull it into lines, directions. I will not go mad. Anne won't go mad. We'll survive.

But no one says that everything is memorable, or rememberable, or necessary to recall. I can't see why I have to think of dead babies. Yes, I do see why: we come from them. Annie and Phil in Maine this summer of their lives were born somehow from two dead babies and the dead motionless air that surrounded them and us from the moment of their nonbirth, on. We planted death seeds. We reaped their harvest. We were the crop. But must I see the blind eyes and blood? And must I hear her grunting, watch her body throb? And must I see her face? And must I, to be sane, go mad with her madness of silence, her biting of lips, her picking at the flesh of her fingers, the tightness of her nostrils and eyesockets telling me how her skin is stretched across her skull and how her head must feel like shattered shell from the labor of confining herself within those shell-like walls? I must be honest. But I must survive my survival. I must not die to live. I don't believe in that. When you die, then you're dead. This is an effort at not dying—at learning, if I can, a way of forbidding *her* to die. Whoever we were, I am talking to you. We meet each other here. We will not die.

Still, I think of babies. And I think of kids we never had. This is not a dream, but a daydream, one I can have whenever I want. I've often wanted, and have often seen it:

90

the wide long field, a tundra, nearly, and the reaches of snow, the pearl of the sky, a blankness over the earth, low sun, the etched branches of leafless trees. Annie is behind me, on a hill that dips to where I stand. She is wrapped in a parka and mittens, like a child. She cries out "Phil, you better bring him back, honey." And bobbling over the snow runs our son, a small brown lump of arms and legs and balaclava, all in dark brown snowsuit, barely able to waddle, he's so swathed. I whistle and he pauses, turns in several clumsy motions, sees me, giggles, shrieks a cry of invitation to pursue, and bobs away, moving sideways as ·much as forward over the snow that meets the sky. His little shadow slants blue, and mine looms behind him, blue, and his little footsteps are edged in blue as I whistle again and take off to bring him back. He is small against the whiteness, and he skates on the snow. I crunch on, my feet sinking deeper into the warming crust. I lift my legs high and kick and move on. Wobbling, he runs. He grows smaller on the snow. I pant and lift and kick and lift again and kick and catch my breath and kick and move on. He turns to see me and shrieks his pleasure. He is tiny on the snow. I stand breathless in his tracks. They are shallow, less in the snow than upon it. I look down my legs to see how deep my feet have sunk. I cannot see past my ankles. He flees on it, I lumber through it, lifting it, lifting and kicking free, being clutched and tearing free to catch him, who by at least the snow is still uncaught. He skates on the surface and I sink. I stand, and he diminishes. I see his future elude me. I stand where I am. He is vanishing; Annie calls behind me, wordless, a string of sounds, a passing music—the music of his flight, small shrieks, has gone ahead. He skates, I sink. I make myself waken from what's not sleep. So that is something to tell you (me) and then move on.

Our house is hidden from the road's descent to the sea by evergreens and thick brush. On the other side, meadows run up several small hills to the church, its little low steeple; the church is a box painted white, a slanting roof, little steeple, a motionless bell. Behind us is a falling barn I must prowl through. The barn, like our house, is scoured by weather, white and gray, made of pulpy powdering wood that I must creosote to keep alive. And I must roof the house, jack it level, paint the sashes, put up screens. How many families must have grown here: the house has grown with their lives, and by standing on the hill between the church and us I can almost count the lives. Like so many families around here they built as they grew. So there's the original salt-box they started in, and then the smaller one built on, to which they moved the kitchen, then the smaller one that's now a shed, and then the little barn attached to that. I can walk from the parlor to the kitchen to the shed to the barn and walk up in time, from the earliest days to now, in a straight line through the sills they built as they grew. It's their history I walk through. I step over tools—I've found a knife that a fisherman used, its spike is worn, the blade made slender from years of cutting away—and into tangles of tired brown rope and puddles of rusted angular nails. We live in the wreckage of their time. We live in our own wreckage too. They died away. The handle of the folding knife is yellow bone. I carry it with me, cracked and bound by brass, heavy against my leg. I remember.

Yesterday we woke to play house. We spoke of nothing that mattered, but shivered in wool shirts and watched the mist rise—the sandy earth like a huge rough animal, steaming. I chopped firewood from damp boards and heavy old logs that were hauled to the house, I think, for leveling it. There is no cellar, just a space beneath the floor where a man can crawl. The logs must be for cutting to size and propping under the floor. At the far right-hand corner, the farthest point of the fourth connected building, the barn, there are boards piled flat to steady the house. Three or four of them, thick ones, and then some slender slabs of stone—and if I look I believe I will see that whoever lived here last stole them from the graveyard up the hill behind the church. I haven't really looked. I won't for a while. So I chopped wood and Annie laid out bread and the instant coffee we bought yesterday. Today we'll have to

92

buy chunks of ice for the ice locker (there's no refrigerator here) and some canned foods, some powdered milk, things that won't spoil. The stove on which we cooked was six feet wide and five feet deep, giant and black, a wood-burning furnace. It heated the kitchen and everything smelled of firs. We glowed, and so did our house. I went outside to watch the smoke feather up, announcing to the bogs and soil and jungle of field that we were home. And then I took the boards from the square wooden well, tied the rope to the rusted bucket, dropped it down. It thunked like a frog off a pad. It came up heavy, it was good to pull. The water was sweet and Annie laughed when I hauled it in, splashing, my pants and moccasins soaked. She told me to carry the bucket next time in my left hand, and she watched me as I heard her and then laughed when I did, and we had our bad coffee, sour milk, burnt bread, in the cool damp kitchen of our new house. We showed our teeth and blew out crumbs as we chattered like children. We watched each other carefully, as if we each were afraid, while we laughed, that the other would stop.

I wonder if the ducklings survived—if they kept the temperature high enough, if someone moved in with a camp cot and old magazines and stayed, *worked* at the eggs. But we had to leave. Dead eggs or not, we had to leave. We had to come here. And here is where we have to stay, dead eggs and all, because there is the ocean, down the road. Unless we build a boat, we're living in our last home.

The part about the ducks is not what I meant when I started. I said narrative, and I don't know if those little spurts of dread dabbed in like drops of paint can count for

93

the telling of a story, how we came and what we did and how we can survive. But maybe so. We had a hell of a good day today. And Annie's been taking naps, and sleeping at night (I hope). She's been sleeping when we sleep together in the same bed. I think she also sleeps when I'm down here. The wind tonight is actually cold, and I swear I can smell the ocean. I don't even know what direction it's blowing in from, and I'd better learn directions soon. Everyone around here talks in north or east, and I can barely remember left. I notice how quickly I wrote on past the part about sleeping together. It's as if I'm embarrassed before you (the *me* of the *us* of Boston and New Hampshire and nine years' edging away from the world and into wherever we're bound for). Imagine being embarrassed before your own history! I suppose it makes more sense than being embarrassed in front of strangers who can't matter as much as the time I (you) have put in at being alive this long.

But Annie's been sleeping. I've been learning to work again. We have enough money for the rest of the summer and a little bit into the fall. There's a state teachers college around here someplace, I've heard, and I'll send them a letter one of these days. Maybe they need a composition teacher or a janitor: equivalent jobs. And the lines on Annie's face are opening, looking less deep, less like an etching of a face. I notice that the groove on her forehead over her nose is permanent, though. No amount of Librium or sleep will make her bony forehead smooth as bone again. She's become her own combat ribbon, her own souvenir. She's a battle flag, and no matter what becomes of us, assuming we live, she'll look like she's fought in a war. Which she has. Which I know she still does.

We had a hell of a good day today, buying things. I made believe the money won't ever disappear. We opened a checking account. We bought her dungarees and sent a check to Bean's for rubber-bottomed boots for her. We bought flashlights and batteries and pounds of nails and gallons of creosote and indoor latex white and tint so she can make her own colors,

94

and staples, insulation by the dozens of yards, and an iron. She insisted on an iron, so we spent twenty-five dollars on an antique that you heat in the fire and thump on the clothes. I asked her why, since she hadn't made anything neat in a year. She didn't laugh, but in the middle of the hardware store (smelling of seed and pinewood, creaking wherever we walked), she said "I'm smoothing things out, buddy. From now on when you look like a pig, you're looking like a smooth one." She and I nodded while the hardware man waited for us to make sense. We didn't make sense, but we nodded like toys and it was a good sixty seconds—which I wouldn't throw away for ten minutes of a hardware dealer's most precious day. And I bought a pointed long-handled shovel for enlarging the pit beneath the outhouse. When I told her why we needed it, she said "I can't let you spend your time shoveling shit." The hardware man turned away. She said "Let's get a toilet put in." I told her we should live the way the house wanted us to. She said "I'm tired of living the ways things want me to." I said we'd see. She said "No, I want us to live *our* way." I said we'd see later on, we'd see. She walked out.

We found a grocery store that sells ice and hauled a giant chunk into the back of the wagon. She didn't talk to me until we turned onto the road that went home. When we passed the church she said "I'm sorry I walked out."

I said that it was all right, she could walk wherever she wanted to, what the hell.

She said "No, I mean it. I can't behave like a child."

I asked why not.

She said "Because you need more than that."

I told her that I loved her very much.

She said "No shit" and then began to laugh and we both laughed until, past the church, she said "There's someone in there."

"Where?" I asked her.

"In the church."

"There's no one in the church. The realtors offered to

95

sell it to us. It's abandoned. I almost bought the church instead
of the house."

"Yeah, well there's someone in the church. I saw someone
looking out the door at us when we went past."

"Maybe a kid or—"

"A man. There was a grown man looking at us."

"Probably the real estate guy?"

"He didn't look like a real estate guy."

"Which would be—"

"I don't know, wearing a sandwich sign that said This
Property For Sale?"

"Right."

"But there's someone in the church."

"We forgot to buy toilet paper."

"Phil."

"I know: there's someone in the church."

"All right. All right. I'll go iron some newspaper for the
john."

So we spent the day making the house our house—
scrubbing walls and planning where to sand the floors and
put gymseal down, and what to paint, what to paper if we
can afford something good looking, where we'd have to take
down plaster and put up gypsum board, drinking beer and
eating Spam sandwiches, getting a little drunk in the afternoon
and falling asleep on the lawn in the sun. It isn't a lawn
so much as not-a-jungle, but I'm going to start our mower
and use the scythe and, if I can keep my fingers—I'd hate
to have to learn another new handwriting this summer—I'll
make us a clearing in Maine and build us a fort. Maybe I'll
write a poem.

The barn in the far field behind us isn't a barn, it's
a boathouse. Although I walked across level land to get there

96

—overgrown, weedy, dangerous with nettles—I saw that from the barn and off to the left (north? east? I must learn) the land slants down, gently at first and then severely, so that a man or, say, two or three men with horses, could pull a small boat down the decline and up a small hill, and then on down the hill to the cove, then float out to sea, thinking enormous thoughts about making something from wood that is bound to survive. I wonder why someone would build a boathouse with a hill between it and the sea. Maybe it's a model of the world. Some world—because near the gentle decline, the hill is torn and toothy with rock, and you can find yourself a height of cliff to get down to be at the sea. Coming up to the boathouse in the early afternoon, I saw sun through its boards—saw through the tilting spread-apart slats the inside and then the far wall and the air on the other side. And yet for all its hollowness, it's strong. There aren't any nails in the wood, or very few in the original working, mostly the place is held together with pegs and sockets, the carvings by knife and adze that men did who know how a house made of wood had to stay. It has stayed. The first wood has to be more than two hundred years old, and I saw the angular nails (some handmade) that came later, and then the store-bought finishing nails, the gadgets screwed into place, reinforcing beams put in with steel where they probably weren't needed, the pools of scrap that seem to grow in the grassy floor, the reins and chains and leather chunks that hang on the walls and block out the bright light that washes in and makes the boathouse brighter-seeming than the field I came through to be there.

Along a width of inner wall—gray and powdering, as old-bone fragile as the bleached outer boards—someone built a bench. It's littered with a broken awl, a wide flat carpenter's pencil half an inch long, possibly sharpened by the bone-handle knife I now carry, and there are scraps and flakes and candle stumps, the handle of a hammer, no sign of its head, and under it all, and under even the rubbing that wind and water and the feet of tiny beasts has done, I found some lines from the plan for a boat. It's a palimpsest: children, I think, have scribbled it, and one man carved the word *Yes!* to its right, and the weather has nearly erased it, palms have laid sweat on its stern, or oil has spilled from galvanized tins long crushed and burned and buried. But it's there to see, it's the hull of a small boat that someone knew would spring on the water as magically as if he—loving his tools, bending to his workshelf in this tilting little house—were to walk himself on the water's top. I don't know boats or anything about them, but his plan is mine. I can't even read what he meant, but I know enough to mean it also. I have visions of driving the station wagon in here and buying hawser rope and towing the boathouse straight, then propping it up and putting in new wood, as little as I can, to make it stand—whenever there's time to spare away from the house: that comes first—and moving in some notebooks and pens, maybe running an entryway in for a 220 wire and setting up a lightbulb and hotplate and cups, dragging in some old chairs, not too much though, keeping it always simple, and working there if I can. If I do some work I think I'll do it there—my home away from home away from home away from home.

As Baker used to say, who screwed my wife on a desperate visit, history is a thing of the past. I believe that he meant it to mean something—that standard historiography no longer worked. He talked about oral history, about rewriting the Marxist revisionists' rewritings of rewritten history, and then he was beginning to talk about existential historiography. I always thought it was the pills—talking about *doing* history, making it happen where you are, then saying how you were when it happened, recreating how you reacted in order to say what the world once was. It must have been the pills, he was speeding all the time before he left. Too bad he didn't leave about one night before he did. My wife would still be a virgin, mostly. Virgins are a thing of the past. And maybe so are wives. Who knows? (Certainly, not the husbands.)

I thought of Baker and his history as I dug up the out-house. It was easy enough: Annie and I jacked it up, slid it onto boards, and moved the whole structure away from its hole. I held my breath and she was almost gagging, but there wasn't any smell, nothing but a sweetness like mildew and dark rich earth underneath. I said "Hey babe: a hundred and fifty years of history down there."

She said "That sure is a lot of shit."

I jumped down into it—my feet slid *down,* I thought for a second I was sinking into the world—and Annie threw the shovel in beside me, like a spear. "Hey warrior queen" I said.

She said "I want to go someplace and lie in the sun, okay?"

"Listen" I said, sweating already, shoveling up to a neat pointed mound at the height of my shoulders. "Listen."

"No, I won't get lost."

"Don't stray."

"When have I strayed?"

"Indeed."

"Hmh?"

"What?"

"You're saying I have?"

"I'm saying please shouldn't. So I can find you when I need you."

Above me, long and slanting, she said "Phil? When have you been needing me?"

"You name it, babe."

"You're so goddam paternalistic, you know that?"

"Of course."

"Of course. Phil?"

"Yes, babe."

"Phil?"

I put the shovel into the soil at my feet and stood beneath her, looking up. I said "Whatever it is, don't worry. You look a year younger already. Not worrying is very good for you. All right? Don't worry."

"You look like you're standing in a grave" she said. She looked past me over the field behind the house, past the bleached leaning boathouse, toward the bogs and jungle meadows.

I said "Except I'm not. This is where *they* dumped themselves, whoever lived here. *Their* grave, maybe, but not mine. Don't worry."

"But it *looks* like—"

"No."

We stayed that way, and then she nodded, then walked off. I stayed where I was. I held to the haft of the shovel with both my hands and looked at where she'd been, at the mound beside me, then down to where the shovel lay buried so that I stood like a scarecrow pried from its pole but still holding on. Then I went back to digging and worked until the sweat was in my eyes and I couldn't see. I kept on clearing that pit out, and when my neck muscles jumped I sank the shovel in again and sat in the shade that the hole made. I leaned my shoulders against the side of what I'd dug and tilted my head back and watched the light come in.

Her shadow broke the light and she climbed down. She said "Have a beer, it's almost cold."

"A grave matter, this beer."

"A shitty pun."

"A shitty grave."

She leaned against the smoothed earth wall opposite me —chopped roots, pink thick worms, the whiteness of rocks —and rubbed her head against it. She said "I didn't want you to be in here alone."

I got up onto my knees to open the beer for us. She jumped when I tore the top from the can. Her work shirt was open to the waist and at the side was pulled from her dungarees. I walked on my knees to her as if I had only stumps.

100

I went to my hands and knees, straddling her long legs as she sat, watching the sweat on her bony chest, moving in. She watched me with her eyes nearly closed. I touched her thigh and she hissed. I kissed her wet hard throat. I said "Okay. I'm not alone."

She said "Oh."

"Did you say 'No'?"

"No."

I sat back up and drank the beer. It spun my head and I panted. I said "But not yes?"

"Not anything" she said.

I nodded. I sat. I drank more beer and gave her the can. The beer was making my throat ache and I cleared it to say "I should go back to work."

"I love you."

"Sentenced to hard labor."

She nearly smiled, but she was crying.

I said "Don't worry, babe."

She said "It's so much like a grave in here."

"Don't worry."

She said "No, I'm not."

A nnie spent the day in the sun, walking around the outside of the house with a can of creosote and a reeking brush. Most of the time she was cursing from when creosote fell on her bare skin. She was nearly naked in an old bikini which she made long ago, so badly that it wouldn't stay on in the water, and she looked all right, though too skinny, walking around the house with her brush trailing after on the wall; she looked like a gawky girl, a kid, somebody's child. I saw the grown-up muscles in her thighs, though, and the mole on her muscled back, the dimple under her ass: my favorite, scariest place on her. When she was born she wasn't breathing,

101

her mother once told me. She was blue and not breathing in, she wouldn't be convinced to take in air, so she was dead. Anne was not a live-born child. The doctor grabbed a hypodermic full of something good—adrenaline?—and jammed it into the back of her thigh. He saved her life but the needle broke off in her body, so while she was breathing he had to save her from the streptococcus invasion that followed. She told me once that her birth jinxed her birthings. Needless to say, I told her it was my famous poisonous seed. At that time of our lives she was saying things like this; she replied "It sure doesn't taste like poison, and I should know," and that was the end of my famous poisonous seed discussion. Now I think again about my poison seed. Still, that fat dimple under her left buttock is a place my hand has sought, would seek. It's where she began. Most people don't show where they began, and you don't need to know, really. But I'm glad to have it, still, that crevice of deathlessness she carries. It's our guarantee. She's my guarantee. I'm hers.

So Annie spent the day painting creosote on, dripping it on her smooth legs and swearing, spattering whatever grows at the sill of the house and killing it off. It won't grow back. I needn't tell her that. Because what she's doing is sealing the wood, keeping dry rot out, protecting the house and making it live. Let the flowers take care of themselves.

I wore a hat from the hardware store—white with black letters I still haven't read: I see no need to read now; I haven't reread a word in this book yet—and I stayed out in the sun. I did a little patching on the roof, which scared me halfway into chatterings: it's so damned steep. I hung on and forked some shingle up and put some tar paper down and even got some units of new shingle on, though there's plenty more to do. But I did some. I can feel the house getting tight. Hanging up there, looking down bright green grass and the dullness of the bogs, seeing the silver of water at the shore below clusters of bushy trees, smelling wind and hearing Annie scratch away with her filthy brush, swearing—it all came into

my head with the sun, the bright aliveness of it all: I closed
my eyes and the house spun underneath me. I was having
too much world, so I came down. There was plenty to do,
there still is, and we are doing for the first time in a year, more.
We are doing, not being done to. And I think perhaps we'll
be all right. She swears like a roomful of men.

Tonight, just now, I went back out to the ladder and
very quietly went up again. The shingles were still warm, but
the air up there was cold, I heard it hissing in trees. I heard
the water over the insects' chirring, and then I saw flames—I
thought at first they were flames, the high flickering embers
of a whole city, dozens of apartment houses gutted to the
beams, still slowly burning. I remembered that the Navy had
its long-range antennas over there, far away, invisible during
the day, lighted at night with thousands of red bulbs to warn
the planes away. It looked like a city destroyed. But it isn't,
I remembered that, remember it now. I turned away from that,
and I saw the light in the window of the church. The steeple
was dark, and the lights in the first-floor windows were dark,
but upstairs, where a balcony might be, or offices perhaps,
there was a yellow wavery light. I came back down. I went
inside, whistling. I said "Kids." I said "Probably kids doing
something they shouldn't. Something like that. A ring of dope
fiends. A black sabbath. Ha ha." Ha ha.

All day the local people have toured us. Because it's
been so dry, we can see them on the high ridge road that
runs from town to the dirt road that runs to our own road—
a trip that's long enough to raise a squall of dust and short
enough for the dust not to rise and fall, but stay aloft: they
come from a cloud, they fall upon us from a sky of brown
dried earth, they dive to our lower world. We see them drift
to us, the sounds of their engines strangled by the dust they

blow up, sun winking on their windshields—their cars are always clean—and they slow, craning, pointing, talking; then, as they come abreast of the house, they look ahead to the sea where the road stops. They say nothing. They look at nothing. There is no empty house no longer empty, cleaned and repaired, no girl in nearly nothing swabs the wood on top of a well not used for twenty-five years, and no tall man on the roof clings, a gargoyle, overlooking their inspection. And then they are past, looking back, noticing the hairy stranger and his impudent glare, the girl who ought to be ashamed—they wonder what goes *on* here at night if this is how they act in the daylight—and they stop and turn around at the cove to come slowly up, looking at nothing, pointing at nothing, until they're past. Then they've seen us steadily and seen us whole.

After the third car (we had at least eight) Annie did a time-honored Anne-of-the-Sorensons rage: as a wide long 1955 Chrysler—grinning chrome, unsmiling face of its driver —drifted past like its dust, Annie stood from behind the well, waved; the car slowed, the driver turned, she lifted a breast from the halter of her bikini and smiled an idiot's wide-nostril smile of glad despair. The car stopped, rocked on its springs, backed up—first going at one side of the road, then threatening to run off the other, as if it were something dizzy—and backed without stopping to the intersection where the driver floored it and the car ran home.

She stuffed herself back in and I said "Have you made us some friends in the town?"

Without turning she said "He didn't act like I was flat-chested."

"Nobody said you were."

"I've been saying it for—a long time. I've been saying it for months."

"I never heard you say that."

"No?"

"Nope."

104

"I must have been quiet about it."

"Well, you're not."

"Flat-chested?"

"Quiet about it. I imagine he will spread the word that you're not. It'll get around. Probably we'll have fishermen coming down on Sunday for the tit show."

"Well it pays to advertise, doesn't it?"

That was in the late morning, and it went like that all day. At least I think whatever "it" was went along the way I think. I mean to say she seemed to me to be reacting to herself out loud, in the world, publicly, instead of shuddering inside the way she did all fall and winter. Yes. I think she's opening out. When we went to town for ice this afternoon she wore my tee shirt over her bikini, and that was all. She's claiming them back, all those men, those secret stirrings, all that static lust, those resentful glances; men give them to anything as naked as she was, anything as wounded and unpredictable as she looked to be. She's never understood it's more her half-mad eyes, her mouth that can flicker, even the brave defiance of her throat—not naked limbs. I walked behind her, not seeing them watch her, missing her watch secretly back. Go, babe.

And late in the afternoon, when we were stiff and salty, we drove to the end of our road—a kind of harbor made of baked mud and high bright stones—and climbed the rock wall before us to look out over scrub and yellow beach at the water that banged in upon us past the abandoned fishery still falling down, slow motion, after more than twenty years. Off to our left, almost invisible, the black steel and guylines of the Navy's radio towers picked up sun. Gulls cried like people, the wind came cold. We sat in jeans and long-sleeved shirts and drank the beer we'd brought in the string bag Annie bought in England for our marketing trips. I thought about England— Chesil Bank, where the stones were amber, perfectly round, and the surf crushed onto the stones and didn't ebb out, sank straight down among the rocks as if the earth had sucked it in. She was terrified there, like a child, and then delighted. We drank Guinness stout and watched the fishermen standing to their thighs in the water while the whole world roared. I thought of the cathedral close at Salisbury, D. M. Beach's bookshop just outside the medieval wall where I bought too many books each week, the books we read at night in the cold cottage, Annie in that old lady's chair like a ghost of her—propped straight, the book in her lap, the light not good enough but sitting in the same chair anyway. And that amber city, Sherborne, where I acted like an idiot at Wyatt's grave in the floor of the small cathedral. We came home from England to start a chain of deaths. Like settlers in the countryside, we got killed off, one by one, one by one. And now we're what we started with, we're the entire dynasty we began. It's worth so many poems, I keep thinking. It's worth one long one: an epic, a domestic epic, yes, the whole world acted out in one little family, damaged and patched, like our house.

Which was more than enough, so I said "What gives, babe?"

She leaned into my chest with her shoulder and said "Lyme Regis. Remember it?"

The Cobb curving out to the ocean, rain and wind that nearly blew us off, and afterward the fishermen in pubs, the people on holiday sullenly drinking tea, clatter of crockery and murmur of voices, the laughing drunken redheaded man who said he came to drink, not fish, and wasn't the weather grand, the tangled bank across the harbor like a mountain of gray-green bush, the long ride home wet and laughing, then Annie sleeping in the car and half on top of me, stopping to buy tinned meat pies, listening to the BBC and drinking supermarket wine—"Duke duh Jorge" she called it; I called it "A resinous claret without pretensions, yet proud of its heritage and not without a certain resonance on the tongue"— and wrapping ourselves in the coarse cheap blankets from Scotland and reading in bed until we fell asleep. I said "I remember it."

106

"We had such a fine time. We were always resting, no matter what we did. Until the end—it was so—such a *clean* easy time."

"It's coming back."

"I don't think it can come back like that. Be what it was over there."

"Good times are coming."

"Hosanna."

"Really. They are."

She said "Would you like another beer?"

"Let's go back and build a fire in the stove and destroy some eggs. As only I can. Eggs and sausage and some sleep."

"You think it'll be—"

"It'll be good. It *is* good. We're good. It's all developing fine, we're all right."

"It's coming along, isn't it?"

"Yup. We made a good move. I'm glad we came."

"Me too. It's getting dark."

"They'll light those goddam towers pretty soon. I hate them. Let's leave."

"I thought we could wait until it was really dark and then we could whistle."

"As in whistling in the dark."

"As ditto."

"Jesus, you're a cynical woman."

"Ask the man who owns one."

"Meaning me?"

"You tell me, buddy."

"Bitch."

"In the hallowed tradition."

"Hey, little girl: Yankee chocolate? nylon stockings? Would you like to be hallowed?"

"Why, how does a little girl get hallowed, mister?"

"Come on back to the car. Come on back down these rocks and back to the car and I'll show you."

"Only in the back seat."

107

"In the hallowed tradition."

"Phil, I feel dry as cork."

"I'll uncork you."

"Phil—"

"Come on."

And we did go back to the car and get into the rear seat and lie on top of each other and giggle like kids. I emptied at once, like a kid—in the hallowed tradition—and maybe she didn't, but she did feel good. She didn't hold herself away. She was learning to be wooed again. She felt glad for herself, and we didn't speak. Later we drove back up, the high red embers glowing on the sky behind us. I couldn't talk and she couldn't either, and maybe she didn't see the yellow light in the church. I said nothing and she said nothing and we went to sleep all wrapped in each other, alone together, snoring on each other's skin. The sun is up in grayness like a ripe peach. It hangs in the dark, it waits for us to start the day. All right. Now we start the day.

This morning we swam around each other like fish, slipping in the smooth water surely, steadily, not touching, not coming close, not staying awfully far away. We didn't speak about what happened on the back seat because nine years of being married had gone on, in and around. And how could I tell her that the rasp of her pubic hair against my belly had felt foreign in the darkness on the seat's rough cloth? That her strangeness excited me as much as the sweat we shared between our bodies comforted me? That I'd felt like a wooer? Felt sorry as a high-school virgin once was supposed to feel? That I'd been done to as much as I'd been the doer? That I hadn't thought of Baker until I woke? That I missed him, hated him, didn't care for his fate? That, when I thought of him, I had snuffled a kind of bashful private sob for her—

108

crazy and hot, spinning like a compass near an engine, lost in her body and sick of her mind, choking in his lusts on his back seat, raging for a victim, a reason, some criminal cause? What could I tell her? I said nothing. And I watched her—she was watching me—work at saying nothing too. But we did smile. We did not radiate fear. There was generosity in the house. It felt warm. Near the windows it looked like Dutch paintings, perfect blues and browns, a brimming sense of tender light. We saw things. We saw each other. We were patient. Nothing, for a while, felt raw.

She said, sitting in my bathrobe, lost in it, small as a child, "I'm staying in today. I'm doing woman's work."

"What's that? I never saw it done. Not since I left home when I was little."

"It's called sweeping. Washing clothes. Doing dishes. I believe I will dust."

"Dust? That's what grows on the road."

"You're as funny as—"

"Yes?"

"I can't think of anything. You bastard." She closed her eyes. "I don't really *feel* like thinking of anything."

I said "But you never dust. It's against your—principles. Yes: dusting is anti-you."

"Well I decided to dust."

"Jesus. Next thing you know you'll be washing yourself."

"Next time."

"Next time what?"

"Next time you snag me in the back of your car, hotshot."

"Oh."

"You're blushing."

"I'm sure I'm not blushing."

"How come your face is turning red?"

"From the sun."

"Oh. Well I'm staying inside to clean."

"Roofwork today. I'll be up on top." I waited for her to smirk or make a joke, but she didn't, and I didn't, and we talked about what I would do and forgot to banter, which was a relief for us both. I wanted to tell her she'd be angry after a while—about acting like a bona fide housewife the morning after whatever it was that had happened; she would look up from dusting a table and she would see herself dusting a table —Hausfrau Being Grateful, Assuming Her Place, Paying Back Her Delight—and she would come outside demanding vengeance, picking a fight, hating me for how she felt (however she felt). And how could I say that?

So I went outside and walked around the house, looked down the back field at the gray-white boathouse, at the trees beyond it, at the meadow that ran to the hill and then the sea. I looked up the hill at the church and tried to see motion there, but it bulked with the sense of emptiness it should have contained. I took half-inch rope and a section of scarred wooden ladder from the barn, then carried the ladder to the side of the house outside the sitting room. I threw the rope up and over the roof, then loaded my coverall pockets with roofing compound, hammer and trowel. I went around to the back, where the rope lay on the ground, and I walked with it backward, hauling, until I felt the ladder come. I pulled and it stuck, and I slackened, then pulled, then pulled more and the ladder went up. When I saw its top at the peak of the roof I kept the rope taut with my left hand, hurled the rest of the coil back at a low gnarled fruit tree; then, keeping the line tightened, I went back to the tree and knotted the rope with half hitches so that the tree would hold the ladder in place. I went back to the barn and got the aluminum ladder we had brought and carried it to place beneath where the wooden ladder hung on the roof. I climbed up, closed my eyes, grabbed the bottom rung of wood and pulled myself up slowly until, climbing almost flat, I was lying high on the roof.

Sun glinted up from the cracked shingles. Sun came off the water and off the glass of the windows of the church. I squinted and worked, deciding not to look around. I worked without going back down for the hat I'd forgotten because Annie was having her own time inside and I didn't want to intrude. I held

110

with one hand and with the other verified what my eyes were after, shingles that were cracked or curling up. We had a leak inside and it would grow, until in the winter the freeze and thaw would pull our roof apart and let everything in. I saw some nails that were loose and I tapped them back into place, then covered them with compound, always holding on. It wasn't too bad. The worst would have to be replaced—I'd have to replace the whole roof pretty soon—but I could do makeshift work for a while by prying the badly cracked shingles up and laying down some metal patch. The roof would hold.

Then, off to my right (north? or east?) I saw one that curled severely. I wanted to pull it up, mark my place for later in the day and also check for damage to the surface below. So I reached off to the right, reached a little more, then wedged my feet in the rung and crawled with the upper half of my body to reach the break. And of course my feet went out. Of course I tried to run them back up into place. And of course I couldn't. The sun rang like music. I was off the ladder, shuffling, crawling, grabbing with my nine fingers, and then I was spread-eagled flat on the roof, hanging on with nothing to hold to, tools falling off, the tin of compound dropping away, very slowly sliding, then slowing, then still, but with nothing to do about staying there, and in my immediate future a fall.

I lay my face on the hot shingles and it burned. I jerked my head up and slipped a little. I didn't move again. I said "Annie?"

There was only the wind through spruce trees and its rustle in the bogs, the sound of a car someplace, a hiss from wind through the jungle near the boathouse, thumpings inside from Annie at her work.

I shouted "Anne?" My voice bounced off the hill and the church and came back. "Anne? Annie? Hey?"

Her voice came up through the roof: "Hey what?"

"Would you come outside, please?"

"What's the matter?"

"Annie, would you please hurry the fuck up and come outside?"

I heard the door slam and I had to shut my eyes again

111

because it rang in my head with the sun and I saw things two or three times. I said "Annie, I wonder if you could come on up here for a minute."

"Are you all right? Phil?"

"No. Yes, I mean. I mean I'm almost all right. If you would come up here and give me a hand."

"I can't see you, Phil. Phil?"

"Here, babe. Up here. Here I am, up here. Just come up the ladder and when you get to the top, reach up as far as you can and you'll feel another ladder. Will you do that?"

I heard her go through the grass and I heard the aluminum ladder squeak, and then I heard her say "I can't feel the other ladder, Phil. Baby, what's wrong?"

"I'm kind of off the ladder and it's kind of steep and my head seems not to be working right, I guess. I think you have to come and get me."

"Oh God. Phil, I can't find the ladder."

"Well that just makes it more interesting."

"Phil—"

"Okay, okay now. You have to get up on the top of the aluminum ladder and reach up as far as you can and squeeze yourself tight and reach up a little higher and you'll feel it. Really, you will. Are you doing that, babe?"

Her voice creaked with her stretching, and I heard her start to pant. "Oh Phil, I can't—"

"Yes you can now. Yes you can. Close your eyes and catch your breath and count up to one, because I'm really slipping a little bit, and reach up, babe, and you'll feel it. Go ahead."

She was whimpering like a child and I heard how much she worked at it and then I heard her breath go out and she said *"Yes!* Okay. Phil? I'm coming up. Right?"

The roof went around under me. I said "Yes, right, right. Yes. Pull yourself up on the rungs now until you're even with me."

She said "Oh God. Don't slip."

"I'm not supposed to slip. Right." I started to giggle and she talked to me, but all I could do was laugh.

She said "Here. Shut up. Here."

I felt her fingers crawling on the back of my left hand and then she was holding my wrist. I said, laughing, "I wonder if I can move."

She said "Move. I'm holding you. Move."

I went sideways while the roof turned around. She was crying more now, and I was laughing more. I moved sideways again and I said "All right?"

She made more noises, then said "You haven't come any closer, Phil. Can you try to come a little closer now?"

I laughed high in the back of my throat and it sounded like a local bird making its little statement. I moved again and her hand closed down on my wrist and there was that pull, steady pull, so that I had a sense of direction even though the roof was going around.

She said "Good boy. Good boy. Once more now."

I did whatever that meant and I felt her other hand on my arm and I did it again, and then I was holding to the ladder beside her, the two of us high over the last place left in Maine, laughing or crying or neither or both, holding onto each other and the ladder, me with my eyes closed tight and everything going around. She kissed my cheeks and my nose and my neck and I started to shake. I said "Too much sun."

She thought that was very funny, and I enjoyed her pleasure so I shouted too. We both made our little statements on the roof, the wind flapped her bathrobe like a sail, the roof turned around, the house sailed through the sunlight, we held on.

And it continued today, a steadily going, holding on. She refused to let me up on the roof again, and I agreed to be refused permission, so we drove into the village early in the morning, bought a styrofoam ice chest, a small cake of ice, a dozen India Pale Ales in their cool green bottles, a pound of prosciutto, a couple of onions and peppers, two long loaves of doughy artificial Italian bread, and we drove onto roads we didn't know.

The car made thumping noises whenever the road wasn't smooth and Anne said "It feels like something's loose."

"Because it is. You win the golden husband for guessing."

"Would it be the wheel? Or would it be something unimportant, like the mizzenmast?"

"It's called the sway bar. That's what I think it is. You feel it at the rear right wheel?"

"Sway bar? Does it matter that we have one? I don't think I ever rode in a car with a sway bar."

"Well, it keeps you from driving off the road. Crashing. That sort of thing."

"And ours is broken?"

"It sounds like."

"Sounds like. Does that mean we'll have an accident today?"

"Would you like one?"

She waited very briefly, then said "You smug pig masculine car fetishist. Knowledge-monger. Sado-knowledge-masochist."

I said "As long as you feel good, babe."

She nodded her head very seriously and looked at the beaches to our right, the flatlands at our left that ran into scrubby hills and shacks with LOBSTER signs painted on. The narrow oiled black road went at the sea. She said, not looking at me, "I feel very good."

I nodded. I watched her hand crawl over the surface of the inside of the car. I said "You need anything, babe?"

She said "No." Then she said "I was looking for wood to knock on."

I dug with my fingers into the crevice at the back of the seat and I came up with a carbon copy of a gas bill. I laid it on the seat and knocked, said "Go ahead, it counts."

She rapped her knuckles at it and said "You're sure it counts?"

114

"Paper's made from wood, right?"

She nodded.

"So it's the same as knocking on wood. Right?"

She nodded. She nodded again, and looked out ahead. I knocked on the paper, but she said, then, "I don't know. Phil. I don't know if they're the same."

I said "Sure. Of course."

She said "I don't know."

I rapped my knuckles on my head. I said *"That's* made of wood all right."

She smiled and tapped my temple, leaned long over the seat and kissed me behind the ear, rubbed my thigh with her wide long hands. She said "You're full of shit," kissed me on the side of my mouth, then went back to lean against her door and watch the gray-black rocks get larger, listen to the *crump* of our broken sway bar as we went over dirty small roads to be some place near the sea where no one else was.

We found the place. We left the car on a small lawn of low blue-green grass near the almost coming-together of two giant mounds of brown and gray and black soft stone. The beach beyond them was wide and white and shaped like a circle, like a harbor made of land; the sea was its shore. Between the rockfalls from the cliffs—the space was like a door—the beach opened out to be smooth and hard and littered with kelp and shells and driftwood. There were pieces of boat that men had been in. There were table legs and even a pot. The tide lines came up to the lawn, nearly. It was a place the ocean owned.

We walked around. We said nothing. In a couple of hundred years of secret sealed-in beach, we drifted, picking up stones and throwing them at the sea and seeing that nothing mattered, it took everything in. We moved separately. Anne would be kneeling at a whorled smooth wood chunk, then, next minute, be halfway up a gentle abutment of the crumbling cliffs, hanging on, long and skinny, and very serious in her play. I went closer and closer to the sea. After a while I stood in

115

the tide, thinking sometimes about Chesil Bank and what it had cost us to leave England and come to America where suddenly everything had offered consequences and they hadn't stopped. I thought about other things too and the water was over my ankles and I was cold. The coldness came as much from what I'd seen as from the water and wind. The cliffs that made a harbor of beach ran out on the flanks and then became shoals. The water came dark green, dark gray, the stones were brown and black and gray, the sky above the sea far out was the gray of the rocks except where the wind whipped whiteness up, and everything seemed sometimes to merge—stone and sea and sky—so that I looked at one immense solidity coming in at us. I looked down at the water coming up my legs, then looked out again and spread my legs and waited, and the wholeness of it—that looming threat of giant simultaneous arrival—ended when something, some fish far out, cut the water against the grain of its tide and marred with its whiteness the picture of total danger. It was just the world again. Annie was skipping rocks across its face.

She stooped to get more rocks, straightened, went up on her toes, pointed, called. Her cry came up on the wind in fragments, but I nodded, pointed too, shouted back. She cried again, pointed at the stark white wake of whatever swam out there, called—it came in bubblings, as through water—"Moby Dick! Phil! It's Moby Dick!"

I started walking toward her through the surf, watching her dance and name it. I nodded whenever she looked at me and kept on walking to her as she rose and fell, naming. She was red and squinting and smiling with her whole face when I came up and put my arms under hers and lifted her up in the air, off the ground, and whirled her like a child, around and around on the beach, her face in my chest, her arms hanging out, her legs spread, extended, spinning straight out as we spun and spun and spun and fell together on the shore.

Later we carried the food and beer to the farthest left (or east? south?) of the beach and climbed over low rocks, then boulders, to where tidepools pocked the hard brown sand. We went on, through the pools, to giant ones, then a stream, then high rocks and the sound of the ocean beating on the other side of them. We climbed onto a flat stone surface and made sandwiches of ham and pepper and onion, opened two ales and put the rest in a tidepool beside the rock. We filled our mouths with spicy pulp and washed it down with the pure cold sourness of the ale, not talking, stuffing our mouths and emptying two bottles, starting two more. With the half-empty second bottles beside us and my pockets filled with onion and pepper seeds, the rinds of bread, we lay on the sheet of gray rock and looked at the metal sky, listened to the tide come in.

Still we said nothing, and then Annie said "There's a cave. Behind us, up there."

Across the stream and over rocks, part way up that side of the cliff's seaward abutment, there was a narrow high opening. I said "I bet you smugglers used it. Probably still do, you know, Yankee shrewdness, beat the government tax people, all that coastal American ingenuity stuff."

"Let's go see it."

"Nah."

"Come on, Phil."

"We don't want to go breaking our legs in strange caves."

"If we get used to it, it won't be strange. Then we can break our legs in friendly caves."

I didn't say anything, and then I said "Why push our luck?"

We sat and looked at the high wet black narrow mouth in the cliff, ocean pouring over rocks beneath it, foaming dangerously, sending echoes back from the black mouth.

She drank some more ale and said "You think we better not, huh?"

"Next time."

"When's that?"

"Whenever we take a day for it and come here and decide it's time to go into the cave."

117

"When's that?"

"When we decide."

"And you don't think we're deciding now?"

I said "No. No. What do you think?"

She looked at me, at the cave mouth, then at me. She drank more ale and said "No. I guess we're deciding no."

"I think so."

"Yes. I guess so. I guess you're right."

We looked at the cave and finished our ale. I said "You want some more, babe?"

She looked at the cave and said "No. Let's take the rest home. Let's go home and have a nap and read and drink it at home."

"We'll come back again."

"Okay. We'll come back another time and go inside."

I said "Next time we'll go inside."

"Next time" she said.

We each carried a handful of green bottles and we helped each other over rocks and across the pools, walking quickly back to the car, not looking at the ocean behind us, or the sky that came down on top of it. Going home, the car limped like something wounded. I drove it too fast.

W hat bothers me most about this is how much I'm tempted to change it. Because now I do look back—which, with my hand, means looking up and to the left—and I see that I've written, earlier, in the first wide-lined notebook, "chiseling the details, I must make what's happening come out of what's happened. . . . I have to organize, pull it into lines, directions." And then I say "We'll survive." Well, I suppose we will. No, I don't mean that. I did mean what I wrote, and what it said between the lines—that we'll come through, if I can help it, and I mean to help it, and now I think that Annie does too. So maybe we'll live. But—and maybe this is because of the poetry, the fact that it isn't coming, hasn't for so long come—I find that I'm as concerned with making whatever this is (diary, journal, "narrative" I called it once, notes for a psychiatric task force) into something more: I want to bend and force and *change* what's happened to us, make it more, or different. And I'm coming to care as much for doing that (or those, or them: the midnight *us*) as much I care about the people I am and we are during the day and those parts of the night we're together in. I live with us and then, at night, I live with them. The day—its weather, our moods, the tones of circumstance—is what makes us. Then at night, I come here and try to make us again. I think that I'm not writing down just what happened. Annie once told me, in the worst winter there could have been, that she thought the novelists lied, she didn't trust them, wouldn't read them any more. I wonder if she would trust me now.

She sees my light at night, she says. She told me she thought it was a ghost in the boathouse the first time she saw the lantern through the window here. Because here I am, a slovenly wing chair with a broken wooden arm, the lantern hung above the work table someone built a hundred years ago, the palimpsest of ship design shining like a motto in the wood. I've made some crude screen windows—narrow-gauge screening and staples to hold it on over the broken glass and bone-like frames—and I come here at night. The first week of coming here, I wrote nothing. No—that impulse to change again—I really wrote a poem, and *then* wrote nothing because the so-called poem was bad, very bad. All that's left is what I remember:

> Bag of death I drag beneath my head
> he names his body, hauling it.

End of remembered poem, and that is all, because I threw it out with the paper trash I burn at dusk in the wire basket. After that, nothing, not even these—notes. And now the notes again, and now the need to change.

I thought to leave out Annie and the church. Then I thought to change it all—but for what? Because I need to change our lives. Because I need—not to note them—but to *make* them. Now I think that I should write it down the way it was. Of course, if I'm not to be trusted, then I will not say it as it was. It feels as if it isn't, almost, up to me. My thumb jumps as I write this, and my childish writing slopes and strains. But this is what I think it was. I was sitting in the parlor, thinking about writing something down, wondering if I should move these notebooks and the lantern here, looking at the old damp magazines, listening to insects, when Annie came down in my undershirt and said "Hi, Phil."

"What's wrong?"

"Huh?"

"Come on, babe. What is it?"

"Do I look like something—*is?*"

"Something is. Come on."

She sat on the low carved table and I looked at her long smooth thighs, brown from our sun here, the blonde hairs gleaming. I wanted not to see her frightened face that tried to seem so brave. She rubbed her cheeks with her long fingers, still dirty with paint and creosote and the surface of our wood. Then she clasped her hands and said "I saw the light in the church again."

"Which we all know is deserted."

"Right."

"Which you don't believe is deserted."

She nodded, then froze. "Right."

"Want to take a look?"

"You mean go inside?"

"How else could we look?"

"No."

"Are you really scared?"

"Really."

120

"Would you like me to look? Alone?"

"You really think I'm a baby, don't you."

"Do I?"

"When you talk like that—fucking right. You're so god-dam paternalistic, you know that, Phil?"

"Oh."

"Don't give me that *oh* shit."

"Would you like me to go over and take a look?"

"Yes."

"All right."

"No! I mean, what if there *is* something there?"

"Why can't it just be someone? You know, a person?"

"Because you keep telling me there isn't anyone there."

"Well, maybe there *is* someone. And if I go and I see there is, then you'll know, and you won't think it's a ghost."

"Why does it have to be a ghost?"

"It *doesn't* have to be a ghost. Just, that's what you're afraid it is."

"Why?"

"Because that's what you're scared of, babe. Come here."

"No."

"I *know* you're not an infant and I promise not to sound smug. All right? I just think you might want to be hugged."

"You're so goddam—sure. Aren't you?"

"No."

"I don't understand it."

"What?"

"What's there, and why you're going, and what you want to do, and everything else."

"I'm going so we know what's bothering us. Because we're entitled to be alone here because that's why we came. You're allowed to sleep in your house without anybody turning lights on in abandoned churches is why. That's all. It's called the Monroe Doctrine. Baker wrote about it."

"Hey Phil? Fuck you."

And she stood, walked past me and then up, and the room

121

was as it had been—except that she had emptied it out, and there wasn't any more writing for that night, and I was frightened too. So I put my work shoes on and took the three-cell flashlight and went—out the screen door, to the well, then left and up the hill to the top, which was bare of trees, cold from the coastal breezes, silent of the insects I'd disturbed. I could see the blinking lights of the Navy towers, like silently burning ruins. I could see the church, phosphorescent in the darkness. I could see its windows dark, its leaning chunky weight over our house. I went there, through blueberry and fern that crushed beneath me, through clouds of tiny insects that came up like a clicking fog and then disappeared. When I came to the door I turned the flashlight on, turned the doorknob—it was more like the door to a house than a door to a church—and walked inside.

It was hot, as if it hadn't been open to the world for a long time. The flashlight showed me no pews, a long littered wooden floor. There were books, probably hymnals, lying there, and sealed cartons, folding chairs, some stacked, some open, and high closed windows on either wall, some flags nailed up that stood for churchly things, or countries I didn't know of. The room funneled toward a kind of stage behind which were no crosses or goblets or pictures—just a smooth plaster wall with a door on each side of the platform. In its center was a lectern. That was all. I said "Hello?" Something burred when I spoke, as if in vibration to the tones of my voice. Something creaked, like wood under weight. "Hello?" Something burred.

I walked past the platform—my footsteps didn't creak, the downstairs floor was solid—and I opened the right-hand door. Out flew nothing, and I rapped the side of my face with my broken hand to pay myself for my infancies of anticipation. Still hurting, I went on, then up the wooden staircase that turned to the right, then right again, then opened on the second floor, where the light was supposed to have been. My flashlight showed me the beginning of an empty floor. It showed a window, and I assumed there were more, but didn't look. Because

122

I backed downstairs, playing the light on my right heel so as not to fall, but looking at no more. I went on down, barely looking any place, hardly seeing the step I stepped down to, feeling with my hand on the dusty wooden banister, hearing my breath, then hearing my heart beating over the sounds of my breathing—they were two separate rhythms, and I stumbled because the harshness of my gaspings and the muffled rapping of my heart confused me, loosened my joints, made me step between the sounds that came from inside. And I ran the length of the empty floor, jumped the three wooden steps outside, leaving the door opened in behind me, and ran through the insect clouds and the sounds of my body inside as the flashlight jumped up into nothing then down to wobble on the grass, as I ran with little control to the bottom of the hill.

Then I stopped. My legs weren't steady, and I had to sit. I tried to stop. I turned the light off, lay back to look at the sky, but couldn't breathe, sat up, shaking and wet with sweat, tried to stop. I stayed that way, and it was a long time before I walked again, whistling nothing, but loudly, for her to hear, and went inside, put the flashlight in the kitchen on the cold looming stove, stumbled back into the parlor, relit the lantern, sat in the chair which I soaked at once with my sweat, called aloud "Go to sleep, babe. I didn't see anything. Go to sleep."

Which is what I mean: how much did I *really* see nothing, how much was panic, how much was the fear I'd pulled behind me when I went through the door? I feared to stay and see. What I felt—that doesn't belong in a narrative pulling our lives into shape. But what I felt, what I felt—well, how much can a thumbless man grasp?

Today I simply walked into the farthest part of the last barn and wheeled the mower out. It still was caked with turf and earth, the right rear wheel still squeaked as it always had.

123

I just opened the crankcase and looked inside—still filled with oil—and tumbled some gas in from the bright red can, made sure the spark plug was linked, stepped back, pulled the cord, and cut the grass in front of the house. It was a very unmetaphysical mowing. All I cut down was grass. I don't remember what I thought about, but I stopped thinking of thumbs, limbs, how open you are to the world when you're cut: I only mowed. When I was through with the front, I stopped the machine, leaned down with my fingers almost under the mower, and raised its height on each wheel so I could cut the grass on the side of the house without spinning rocks up into my face/ or ruining the blade on stumps. And all I did was lean and adjust, step back again and start the machine—no significant thoughts, no stirrings, nothing sudden or loud. I worked and the work got done.

The reason I say this now—a good cold night, the bugs are down because of the wind, the lantern is waggling and the light's not good for writing by, but fine for thinking of what to say—is that I'm feeling good. This morning I woke and lay in my sleep as it steamed away from me into the day like sweat drying up. My stomach was tensed for the catalogue of troubles, and I waited for the back of my neck to stiffen with what was wrong. And nothing came. Annie was beside me, her mouth open as usual—she looked like an idiot when she slept—and she was belching up her usual snores. But she was lean and brown and soft enough for me to touch—I did it—and feel her coil around the touch—she did—like a cat. It all was pretty good. The bright white light lay against the windows like the purest kind of water. Winds were cool, the swallows in the barn and on the clotheslines throbbed and chuckled, somewhere on the coastal waters someone in a boat decided to lean on the whistle and grunt a jazzy rhythm to the gulls I could hear that circled anything that moved on the sea in case it poured forth food. Everything was in place. The State of Maine was giving what we seemed to need, and we seemed to be doing what we should: taking—with gratitude—and taking again. I leaned over Annie and licked at her ear, slipped my hand up under my tee shirt that she wore and said "Prepare to get congratulated."

He says he's run away. He's over sixty at the very least and he says he's run away. Which is just what we need around here—not only someone else's problem, but the kind we can't do anything about. I don't know. I don't really know if it's funny or not. I think it's not. And I wonder why it had to happen to us. I think we've given to this particular cause. We gave at the office, at the house, at the house before that and the house before that. We gave a hell of a lot, actually, and we'd like to keep a little for ourselves.

I had just come in from scything, which isn't an easy job when you're missing a thumb, and I was wet all over, heaving and huffing, waiting for a little sympathy and hoping that the ice cake had made it through the day to keep my beer cold. Annie was sitting at the swaying kitchen table, leaning her elbows on its ancient smelly red-and-white oilcloth, looking out the little window over the back fields where I'd just been working, and past them to the boathouse and the farthest hills—blue and yellow and blue-green, now—where tree limbs danced and high wild grasses were being combed by the dusk winds rising. She wore faded jeans and a navy blue polo shirt, her hair, still drying, was pulled straight back on her head and tied with a dark blue cotton rag. Her brown feet were bare. Her brown cheeks were white where her hands had pressed them while she watched me slash and bang the scythe off rocks, grimace, flex the pectorals while trying not to pant when I saw that she was watching while I tried not to show that I saw. Because (I said this yesterday: it's important) things were getting *good*.

I said "Hey, babe."

She said "How sure are you about the church, Phil?"

125

I turned around and walked out. I came back in. I said "Hi, babe."

She looked at me, looked at the table, said "You really think I'm a pain in the ass, don't you?"

"I think when I come in all tired and heroic from the fields, I want to talk about me, not the church."

"Well, I'm worried about the church."

"It'll be all right. Churches can take care of themselves."

"Hey Phil—"

"Okay. Okay. We'll talk about the church. Can I have a beer?"

"Can you remember where we keep them?"

"Ooh. This is more or less a nasty one, huh. I mean, we're heading into white water, it feels like."

She held her face in her hands so that I couldn't see it. She mumbled out between her fingers "I saw a shadow there. I saw someone moving upstairs." She took her hands away and I saw that she was blushing. I hadn't seen her blush for a long time. Her tan turned darker brown. She reached behind her to the ice chest and opened it, got us each a beer, even opened mine to apologize. Then, looking over my shoulder, she said "I really think I saw something there."

"God, you look beautiful."

"Oh, shut up. I'm talking about *spooks!*"

I put the beer down on the oilcloth my forearms peeled away from as I stood. I said "Let's go."

"To the church?"

"Let's go while it's light and cover every crack and board. We'll go together, we'll hold hands like the kids in those old movies—Phil and Annie meet the Creature."

"Yeah, but what if we do?"

"Then you'll be right."

"I didn't say I wanted to be right."

"You always want to be right."

So she stood up and slammed her beer down hard and walked out of the house, away from me and up the hill, and

126

fast, and I had to really move to catch up—or nearly: I stayed a little behind so I could watch the velvet swing of her ass in those tight dungarees—and we went up the hill from our place to the empty church.

Light on the windows was blinding, and it made the windows glare like blind staring eyes. Everything looked closed. But at least I finally knew that if dusk was coming, and the windows were vessels of light, then west was off behind the house, down near the sea, and east was the church, I could steer by that. As doors are supposed to swing in empty buildings made of wood and abandoned on hills in desolate places, the door swung open as she touched it, and—barefoot, slinky, more and more mine, or at least not anyone else's—she stopped, waited until her back touched my chest, took my hand. I said, in the darkness of the long littered room, "Annie and Phil Meet the Soulsuckers."

"Shut up."

"You see anybody leaping out at us?"

"Shut up, Phil."

Light from the western windows lay on the podium, the scattered books, the brass knob of the door to the left of the stage, the bottom of the door to the right; the light made the room into boards and debris and nothing more. It was less silent, even, than before, and I felt sad for its shabbiness and desertion; until we had come, I had never heard of abandoning churches. And then I remembered how we had moved from our rooms into other rooms, leaving each other behind; I remembered how we had moved from houses, and from the cottage on the Salisbury Plain and how, as if the houses were stepping stones in a wide filthy stream, we stretched our legs and walked, from one to the other, and kept on moving, and hoped. I thought of churches abandoned, of houses left behind, of offices not worked in, gardens not kept, children not born, not even conceived, and I felt—in dusty tangerine light, in someplace that no one came to any more—how hard we had to work, now, to stay where we were. I didn't know if after Maine and

127

the rocks and the sea there was any place left we could go except Europe again. I had the feeling that as soon as we got there someone would die.

Annie said "What's wrong?"

"Nothing."

"The blood was jumping in your hand, it was twitching."

I took my hand away, wiped it on my shorts, put it back for her to grip. She did, and I said "I'm okay."

"Really?"

"Really. How are you?"

"Let's keep holding hands." She giggled. "These places spook me."

"Churches?"

"No. Places like this."

We went on. The floor didn't creak, there was plenty of light, although it was mellowing, turning the color of fungus and the golden rot in fallen trees, and nothing announced itself—we feared, like children, that something would come for us to deal with. We had dealt with enough. We were dealing with enough. Only nothing would suffice.

I said "Last time, I went up the stairs in there, behind the door."

She headed for the door, still holding me, I still holding her, and she said "Why do you suppose it's deserted like this?"

I said "There are gravestones behind it, up near the blueberries there. I think the old people died, most of them. Maybe the pastor died. I guess the kids didn't keep coming. And not too many people are moving into the neighborhood."

She giggled again, like a child, as we walked up. She said "It's a little dark here."

"It's getting to dusk. It's a little dark everywhere now."

"Here seems darker."

"Nah."

"Not a little?"

"Nah."

"Bullshit."

"Double bullshit."

She said "You argue as badly as me."

"I."

"Bullshit."

That got us past the turnings of the stairs and up to the landing and into the looming high loft of the second story. It was shadowed and hot, and nothing echoed. We stood still and looked into the dark. We were holding each other pretty hard, and I was looking for something witty, or incisive, or funny, or even dumb—a word to pop the bubble of our tension spreading over everything now—and from the far end of the room, in the darkness I couldn't penetrate, came "I hope you don't mind."

Annie clamped her hand in mine: I had been holding her, but now she was holding me, and she didn't gasp or hiss—she sighed. As if she had been expecting this, at least waiting for whatever this was: she sighed, she sounded somehow relieved. I tried to squeeze back, then said, very low, as if I were calm, "Hello?"

The voice came from the far right rear of the room: "Hello." It was very tired, its deep fatigue made it shallow, like a breath taken with pain. The voice said "Hello. Don't be scared."

Annie said "Are you all right?"

I said "Why did you ask that?"

"Because he doesn't sound it" she said. "I don't know. Being up here, you might not be all right."

The voice said "Thank you."

Annie said "We're not scared."

The voice said "Good."

"But *are* you all right?"

"Thank you very much" the voice said. A light came on from a small flashlight or electric lantern and its suddenness boomed in the dark. I saw clothes and green canvas and white ankles over brown shoes. The light jumped and turned from us and a face floated in the corner: white skin with darker

129

stretched pouchings under the blue eyes, a bald head with fringes of white hair grown long, a smile of embarrassment and loss, yellow teeth. He said "Here I am."

Annie said "We've been seeing your light."

"I thought you might, yes. I guess I frightened you. I'm sorry."

"No" I said.

Annie said "You're goddam right we were scared. Are you all right?"

"Sure. Sure. Would you like me to leave?"

She said "We don't own the church. This is my husband, Phil. Phil Sorenson. I'm Anne Sorenson. We live kind of next door."

"Yes" he said. "I've seen you. I was here when you moved in. It looks like good living there."

We stood, the light leaned off to one side, then tightened back to his face. I said "You don't have to hold that there."

He said "No, I guess you know where to find me. Have you told anyone about me?"

I said "What do you mean?"

Annie said "No."

"Because people might be looking for me. I don't know why they'd look here. Even any place in the state, really. But—"

I said "Cops?"

He laughed, a warm deep laugh.

Annie said "No. We never mentioned the lights up here."

He said "I read at night. I tried to hide the light under my poncho, but it got too hot if I read long. And the bugs were all over me. No, Mister Sorenson. Not the police. Maybe —I don't know, really. I don't think so."

Annie said "It gets dark up here earlier than outside, doesn't it?"

"It seems to" he said.

Annie wasn't holding my hand. She said "Can we help you?"

130

He said "You don't mind?"

She said "No" and she waited, so I said it too. She said "Maybe you'd like a bath and some hot food?"

"I've been cooking on a Primus stove" he said. "Dehydrated beef stew, that kind of thing. I even packed some Army surplus rations in here. I've been eating pretty well. I lugged a little table and some chairs up here. I'm doing all right. I'm doing all right."

She said "You sound out of breath."

"I'm always out of breath."

I said "How did you get here?"

"I packed in."

"You *walked?*"

Annie said "We don't have to really know all that."

"I didn't mean to ask *all that,* babe."

"No," he said, "that's all right. I'm running out of stuff anyway. I'd have had to make some kind of move soon. Yes —could I borrow your bathtub?"

She said "It's yours," and she sounded very glad. She sounded as if she'd expected him—or someone, something— and she sounded ready to do things she'd known she would have to do. So I made glad noises too, and we told him to come on over when he wanted to, and he said he'd see us soon, and we walked to the stairs and went down.

He called "My name is Abe. Is that okay with you? Just Abe right now?"

Annie shouted "Sure" up the steps as we fumbled down. Her voice was high, excited. Then we didn't talk all the way down the steps and through the main room and out the door into the fallen dusk.

In the blueberry bog I said "You were waiting for this?"

"No. I mean, I knew something was on its way."

"Why?"

"Because. It felt like it, I guess. I don't know. I knew there was somebody up there. After a while, I did. And I don't mind. Do you?"

"No, babe, no. Just, I thought you wanted to hide out."

"We *are* hiding out."

"With somebody else."

"Well."

"I think I'm jealous."

"Of *what?*"

"Well how the hell would I know?"

"Of course" she said. "But I wouldn't know, would I?"

"I don't know. You knew about Honest Abe."

"Oh, Phil. Now don't be mean. He's an old guy running away from some place, that's all. We can't say no."

"To what?"

"Whatever."

"Oh."

At the kitchen door she said "I love you."

"Goddam well better."

"Big shot."

"Goddam right."

"Okay" she said. "We'll give him some soup or something and if he's a pervert or a murderer or something you can kick him out."

"Thank you. You're nuts."

"You wouldn't have it any other way."

So now it's late and I'm in my boathouse, Annie's in bed, and Abe—clean and fed, and about to *happen* somehow to us and our house—is back in the church, reading. If I stand outside in front of my window I can see a slice of the light he's turned on. I ought to find out what he reads. That tells you plenty—as when I found out Annie *wasn't* reading: she wasn't reading novels, she wasn't reading plays, she wasn't reading poems. She was reading biographies, the lives of other people, facts about being alive, then dead. Maybe he's a life for her to read. I don't know what she wanted, except maybe lives that were done, patterned and put away, easily managed, packages of problems solved by not living: surrogate suicide. I don't know. But there's something in Abe for Annie. We've

132

played so many fish on so many lines, the lines have been so strung out, and taut, and breaking; we can play one more.

He's a funny kind of man. For all his equipment—and he's got the best I've ever heard about—there's something to him that contradicts the Bean's and Eddie Bauer gear, the AMC maps and Primus stove and lantern, the little polished carbide lamp, the netting, the down-filled sleeping bag that hardly weighs at all, the Norwegian frame pack. For instance, his shoes: low-cut city shoes, expensive, pebble-grain brown shoes for businessmen. His shoes put him in Boston or New York. So do his skinny ankles. His gear puts him up on Mount Katahdin, nothing less than the bad east face. Well, I guess that's what you look like when you run away. He's on some trail away. And he's nothing less than sixty—almost in shape, yet almost sick, and probably over sixty years old, and running away like an adolescent, or a literary backwoodsman (the kind that talks about Thoreau and doesn't necessarily read him). He's polite, he's even shy—and yet he knows too much to be very shy for long: sitting with us after his bath, wrapped in a couple of towels and smoking cigarettes and coughing, shaking his head at the bite of the smoke, conscious of our sense of his body, so not moving very much, and yet knowing that his body couldn't matter for long, giving off the sense of knowing very well what having an aging body implies. He has strong neck and shoulder muscles, short strong arms, a pot but that's recent; his legs are skinny but muscled, his calves too thin. I wonder how it carried him from where he's come, all that recent fat and sag and wither, the gnarl at the neck, the body that once could have walked for days with bad food in bad weather: a businessman who once thought he'd wind up a mountain man. Is he running away to the mountains again? Maine is the place, it's got rocks and pitch enough on Katahdin for any final test, it's got ocean enough around its edges to tell you this is the end, here's where you stop. Or is he running from the city, a huge pack on his back and no place really to go?

133

There's only one road here, but he's made it seem like two. This is the intersection, where the lights hang winking red like embers, the insects scream, the ocean bangs at the rocks, our final house. His road crosses here. I wonder where we're going. I wonder how to say, for Annie, me.

W e didn't see him all that day, and I didn't talk about him. We worked. The work was not a part of our lives any more, it *was* our lives: replacing clapboard or drinking at the beach, wrapped in a plaid blanket together, finishing the roof—this time with a hat on my head and Annie right below me on the ladder, useless and supporting. We did what we'd learned to do, and Annie looked fine. In the late afternoon we drove in for ice and food and a case of beer. When I looked at *The New York Times* in the rack, a day and a half old and flabby with moisture from the sea, it looked like a paper from Italy or Spain. When we came home I chopped more wood and we built up a fire in the huge wallowing black iron stove; on one hole I fried hamburger, and on another Annie cooked asparagus, and we sang *Frère Jacques, Frère Jacques* while we shuffled our bare feet on the dirty worn wide boards and sweated in our old moldy kitchen and the beer got cold on the big clear chunk of ice. While we were singing I realized how little we had said all day. I listened back in my memory as if it were a long dark corridor with a light at the end and I listened to where we'd started the Maine trip, and what we'd said since—I listened, too, to what I'd said we'd said—and I heard how little in the past few days we had talked about troubles. Even in our shifty sidling spooked-up jumpy way we'd said quite little. And in bed, lying alongside each other, sometimes touching and sometimes not, bouncing on the almost sprung springs when one of us moved, reading by battered kerosene lamps in the small bedroom that was dark and screened

134

and cool because of the sea winds, hearing each other and the pages and the insect chatter, the scratch of pine twigs, scream of mouse pursued by owl, the tireless complaint of a mourning dove (its senseless mooing call to nothing about nothing), feeling the furniture around us—always a little damp, but solid and well used: tested—and feeling our house tighten up like a strong hand making a fist, I said "We've been here a while."

Annie was reading a withered *McCall's* about plastic surgery for the average girl. She hummed to tell me she heard.

I put down a paperbound copy of *The Elements of Style*— "A basic structural design underlies every kind of writing. The writer will in part follow this design, in part deviate from it, according to his skill, his needs, and the unexpected events that accompany the act of composition"—and I dog-eared the page, shoved the book under the bed where I wouldn't kick it when I woke and stood, said "It feels like getting pretty good."

She threw the magazine at the end of the bed, it missed, fell, thumped, unwound its folded pages. She clasped her hands on her stomach and made a face like an attentive monkey, said "Speak."

"I am the ghost of Christmas past." I turned my light out, lay back, waited for her to do the same. She did, and she lay back very still, and we both were listening.

She said "You better not be, buddy."

"That's what I mean," I said, "I don't feel any ghosts around. The one in the church turns out to be a sixty-year-old flower child, and the others got lost some place in the woods or back on Route One near the tourist hotels. It's feeling pretty good."

She turned onto her side and pushed her bottom into me. I curved so we'd fit, and we lay like that. She said "Yes. We feel good. We do. Except I don't think we should discuss it."

"No, I didn't mean that we should."

"We'll just live here. Wherever."

"What do you mean, wherever?"

"Wherever this is. Wherever we go."

"Babe, I don't think there's any place for us to go now. I think this is it."

After a while she said "We've had so much happen to us, you know? We did so many things. We had a long winter in the old house."

"I forgot a lot of it" I said. "I forget these things. It's so easy after a while. I feel like we're on the longest vacation. Except we're working. It's the best damn work we ever did. And you were sketching."

She moved away a little and I hugged her back into my curve so we fit again.

I said "I wasn't snooping."

"I know."

"You were sitting back there half naked and making pictures of the boathouse."

"The curve of the field it's on."

"You looked beautiful, babe."

"It felt beautiful. What's that?"

"The famous gristle of the famous side of beef."

"God. *Two* famous gristles."

"Laid end to end."

She said "Let's get laid end to end."

I said "I wanted to ask you—"

"No," she said, "let's not have any asking."

"Just gristling?"

"Just boning up."

"How about boning in?"

"How about that" she said.

"No questions asked."

"Just answers" she said. "Like this one."

"This one?"

"This."

136

I haven't written down here what he said when he bathed and ate and smoked cigarettes in our house, wearing a towel and his city shoes of pebbled grain, sitting in the kitchen with us while Annie paid him attention she hadn't given anything outside our small world for more than many months. It's his voice that's hard to pin down more than it's difficult to remember what he said. He said little, it's true, and what he said was pleasantry, or meant to elude us. The pleasantry I forget, and the evasion I dismiss. He didn't tell us who he was or where he came from or what he was aiming at with his knapsack and gear and burrowing into the corner of an abandoned church at the edge of the country. But it's his voice I find hard to remember. At times, when he was talking of children or animals—or talking to Annie about almost anything—it went deep, below his larynx, and resonated, took on tones of soothing. When he spoke to me, or talked at us in an effort to say nothing about where he'd been and where he was going, the sounds came out of his throat, high and hard, sometimes nasal; he sounded like a good lawyer, feisty and faithful to fact.

The day after Annie and I took refuge in our skin to avoid discussing Abe, I tried to work but couldn't work well. I went up onto the roof and came down too tired too soon, too soft beneath the heat. I started to shim the corner of the house where the gravestones were stacked, but they defeated me. I got the jack on a fairly level rock and pumped it around until it had the weight of the house on it—the sweat was pouring off me like oil and I stank at myself in the wind that blew off the sea and over the hill, past the house and church— and then I pulled the headstones off one at a time, they were far heavier than they looked, and I laid them out in a row. My arms were shaking with the weight of the wafers of stone. I couldn't read anything on them, and the sun rang off crystals in the rock and dazzled me, made me feel weaker. They were very very old, they were far from the bone and flesh-shreds rotting they had once been mounted to guard, commemorate, recall: the pains removed from the wound. They were here and telling us of death and partition, infinite sorrow, and yet they were unconnected to anything but our leaning home, and the grass around it which Annie had burned with her creosote spills. I felt as if I looked at orphans. I cut a wide hunk of post and wedged it in beneath the jacked-up corner, then slammed it into place as hard as I could and unwound the jack.

After I carried the jack to the barn and put it away I trundled out the old wheelbarrow that had come with the place. Its handles and frame were scoured and dry as the house, its metal was rusted and pitted and light as wood after years of corrosion. I don't know why. I tied a rag from the barn around my forehead so the sweat wouldn't run in my eyes. I stood and looked at the stones and breathed deeply, until I felt dizzy with the oxygen rich in my blood. And then I spread my legs and groaned as if it hurt and then arched my fingers, reached for the edges of the leftmost stone, and pulled, hauled it up and over the side of the barrow and in. It sounded unimportant, scraping into the bottom. I did it again, and I did it again, and I did it again. My legs were shaking, but all I did about that was walk back into the barn and take a long-handled spade, wedge it into the barrow, whoop for more air, bend my knees, pull the barrow by hanging my arms straight down and letting my thighs take the weight, then swivel, push with my shoulders, and wobble-march off, behind the house, around it, left, then straight at the boathouse, then left again—over stone and rubble of piping and wood scraps, mounds of earth and ruts of grass—and off at an angle that took me slightly downhill, then faster downhill, away from the house and the boathouse, downhill faster, until I was pulling back with my arms and shoulders, digging with my heels to stop my descent. I went through bramble, hawthorn, the purples of wild chive, under low wide white pine branches, pulling back and gulping loud, no longer steering so much as avoiding. It leveled for a stretch at the base of the little hill beyond which the rocks and ocean rattled. Sea smell came up to the small pine forest I was in, and that was where I stopped. I said "I can't" and I couldn't: the hill was too high—anything was too high, I was finished. So, before my muscles could start to rest, I pulled the spade from the barrow and, making mewing noises like a child alone, I dug in the floor of brown rotting needles, stabbing with my leg at the top of the shovel, leaning down and in with the weight of my whole body, pulling back with only my back and hands because my forearms almost were through. I did that, I dug, and I made a hole big enough by not stopping. As I worked the work I hadn't thought of doing that day, I saw what I had wanted to achieve: me on top of the small cliff over the sea, sliding the stones down one at a time, the sound of their crack and splinter coming up with the foamy wash of the ocean that received their fragments from the rocks. But I dug without a thumb and I finished it, listening to the hoarse shallow weeping noises which were what my body sounded like as it tried to breathe. And then I went back to the barrow and hefted it up—it felt easy this time, and the pain in the small of my back felt more like something outside me but fastened on tight—and I pushed it to the edge, tilted, balanced the barrow on its nose, then grabbed the bars underneath it and yelled and pulled at once: the stones slid out, I fell, the barrow danced to the side and also fell, and it almost was done. I stood and pulled the barrow straight, pushed with the shovel —I almost couldn't hold it now—until the stones were under a mound of needles and soft black earth mixed in with sandy mean soil the forest's own compost hadn't enriched. And then I sat where I'd stood. I let the shovel fall away. I slowly lay back, a leg on the mound I had shoveled; I looked at the sun that danced through the needles overhead when the sea winds blew, and I closed my eyes. There was nothing to think. The muscles in my forearms spasmed and my fingers felt too thick to close into fists. The muscle in my right thigh jumped, rested, jumped, jumped twice. I listened to the winds, to my panting, to the silences around my little sounds. I'm writing this down as truly as I can now, in a cloud of bugs by the light of my boathouse lantern. I can hardly hold the pen because my hands hurt. Everything hurts. But I'm very happy that I buried the headstones and I don't precisely know why, and I think that's all right. It still makes a sense to me that I did it. It still makes sense to write that down. It feels as if there's order in the saying it. And I don't mind not making poems again tonight. I never believed in the writing of lives over art; poems matter most and I'll always believe it. But for me to even have said what I did is a little triumph, and I said it right, I think, and it makes a kind of sense in the sequence of our lives, and I think there's art in that as well. It isn't a poem, but it's somehow sane now while it wasn't when I did it. And that is what's all right.

Because—this is confession—I was already saying it to myself when I came home, trying not to stagger. I was already putting it together as if it had been a single act of will or need, and not a series of stuttered desperations. I was as interested in making a shape of what I'd done (an object crafted in a bleached lonely boathouse at night) as I was in the fact that I had acted mad, crashing through forest and fields with a load of stolen tombstones that had crazily propped my house. I didn't act so I could say it. But already I was forgetting why I'd done the action, and was worrying about the arc of its form, how to sketch it here as I've done.

I couldn't find Annie after I'd put the wheelbarrow and spade away, but I didn't look very hard. I went inside and I lay on the floor for the sake of my back, and in the cool kitchen, hoping that I'd sleep, I fell asleep. She found me there, she woke me with her foot, saying "Hey. Hey, are you all right?"

"I'm not hurt" I said.

"I didn't say you were."

I looked up at her—she wore the top of her bikini and a pair of dungarees—and I said "What a nice-looking way to be wakened."

140

"Why did you say you weren't hurt? What hurts?"

"Don't be smug."

"What hurts?"

"Nothing. My back a little, I was shimming the house and I pushed wrong. Something. I'm okay."

"Really?"

"Honest."

"Don't be noble" she said.

"No" I said.

"Is your back really all right?"

"Stiff. A little stiff. That's why I was lying here."

"You should take a hot bath."

"I will. Will you rub my back?"

"Aha."

"I mean for health. Don't accuse me of trying for pleasure."

"As long as you don't enjoy it. Okay, I'll cook the water up."

So I ran cold water into the tub and waited for the water she was heating on the stove, stood naked at the side of the tub and stared out the window at the boathouse in its field of blue-green grass. From the kitchen Annie called "I saw Abe. I went over to see if he needed anything."

"He interests you, huh?"

"I don't know—yeah. He does. I don't know why. He makes me very sad."

"Did he need anything?"

"He mentioned he had a wife who died."

"Is that why he's here?"

"I don't know. He really didn't want to say. He was sorry he told me, I think. How's your back?"

"No sweat, don't worry. What else did he say?"

"I don't know. It's hard to remember. Isn't that funny? I talk to him, but then I don't remember what he says."

"Me too."

"Me too."

She came in naked with the water for my health.

Day tried not to come. A woolly fog lay around us—we were a ship becalmed—and nothing moved, we were surrounded by a bright darkness, sun making the fog look hot and lighted up, pearly, but not much light coming through to our side of things. We heard insects and the decoy-noises of a catbird, the piping of swallows from our barn, the hoarse high cry of gulls; we sat on the steps outside the kitchen door and drank our coffee, leaning onto one another, and looked into the mists and shadows, waiting for the sun to burn the fog away. It didn't. The day grew warmer, muggier, the sun on the other side of the fog was harder to look at, and the house seemed more and more like a stranded ship or an island we had landed on. So we decided to keep the doors closed for coolness, draw what curtains and blinds we had, and work inside.

Annie was downstairs making a countertop extension in the kitchen; it was very elaborate, with hinges and brackets and other heavy hardware, and it was to double as a work table as well as a counter we could cook on. There wasn't any rhythm to her work, no sense of progress being made, the sounds that came upstairs from her—hammer clacking, the groan of the saw, nails being punched into wood, a screwdriver slipping from the head—were forced and effortful, and she swore as much as she clattered the tools. But I knew that she would get the counter made because she wanted it, so I stayed upstairs and sanded wallboard I had some days before put into the bedroom. I was doing the fine sanding where the tapes were when Annie came up to the landing—it was square, and three bedrooms opened off it—to say that Abe had dropped by, did I want to come down. I was listening to a girl who called herself Lady Jane, the voice of Maine, coming at you with the top forty after one more word from Irving Smith, manager of the motor car company named after three generations of Smith, who personally would see to it that you paid no more for your new Smithmobile than you absolutely had to in order that the little Smiths didn't starve. Over the radio's sound I said "No. How's that?"

142

"Come on down."

"I don't want to come down. I've got this work to do, you tell him, okay?"

"No."

"You're *forc*ing me?"

"Why don't you want to come?"

I rubbed the sandpaper into the wall too deep and scratched it. I stopped so as not to ruin my work and said "Because he's like mail from home when you don't want mail from home is why. He reminds me of the world. Coming into my house—the world blowing in like rain through the windows. That's why."

She leaned back, holding to the railing, and she looked about fifteen years old. "And I kind of am interested in knowing him? Would that be—something?"

"You mean am I jealous?"

"Well—"

"Yes."

"But didn't you *want* me to look at the rest of things? World? Isn't that what you wanted last year?"

"Yes."

"So."

"So."

"Things get kind of turned around, don't they?"

"No," I said, "we're just becoming each other again. It happens now and then."

"Will you come down and we'll talk about it later?"

"Yup."

"And we'll talk about it later."

"Yup."

"And will you stop talking like goddam Gary Cooper?"

"Yup."

Which is why Annie and Abe and I were sitting in the back parlor—dark, cool, furnished with two damp day beds and a lot of needle-point rugs and smooth wood floors I had stained and a picture of Lucky Green going to war which Annie had framed and hung—and we were drinking beer (warming up fast because the ice was nearly gone) and watching Abe smoke cigarettes, him on one day bed, Annie on the floor leaning her back against the bed I sat on. We all were in the room beyond the one I used to write in before I came to the boathouse, and a notebook—speckled, black and white, like a kid's book waiting for school—was in my sight while we talked or sat in silence and learned about Abe.

He said "So when I came in and heard the radio it was like being back in Washington. The President just invaded. But it's not invasion, it's *incursion*. So what do you do? Do you say something? Do you call up a friend and say Hey Hymie he did it again? Nah. You know what you do?" He flicked ash and put the heel of his right foot on the day bed, leaned his cigarette hand across the drawn-up knee. "I'll tell you—look around. Huh? Right. You look around. You check out who's looking at you. Because somebody sees you look bad, it gets mentioned some time casually to someone else, he mentions to someone else Abe isn't happy with incursion for protective reaction, somebody else hears Abe marched in a picket line or signed a petition for impeachment, and Abe is out of luck. It's really much more subtle than that, but it's true. Which is what counts, huh? So believe me you spend a lot of time looking around."

Annie hardly listened. I could tell from the stillness she sat in—like a shadow that lay around her—that she was watching, changing him into stroke and shapes to deal with in her time and in her terms. She was watching the rest of the world. I said "How long did you spend in Washington, Abe?"

His white strong friendly face was a mask, because as he named the cities and times, nothing of their weight lay on his skin or moved his muscles under the jowl or lip. He said "Oh I don't know. Forever. No, seriously, uhm, about fifteen years. Yeah. I was on the fringes of the Vietnam thing since it started with Ike. Before that, I was counsel to the Treasury people in Baltimore and Philadelphia, I did time in New York on liaison with UN drug security and counterfeiting—nothing exciting,

144

just filing papers for people who didn't speak the language. Interpol it's called. Big deal. You know I never saw a gun as long as I was there? And that was at the beginning, when they thought something would happen. Nothing. We all had fattening lunches and worked too hard."

I said "You're a lawyer?"

He said "Used to be." He lit a cigarette and tilted his head back to watch the little puffs he blew drift up, to where smoke already hung in corners and lower down, like a layer of cloud in the house. We were matching the fog outside. He said "I don't practice any more." He smoked and we all sat, I bent the middle of my empty beer can and the noise made Annie jump. Abe saw that and smiled. "I was doing conference work at the end. I was liaising on stuff for the Army PX shipments over there. You know about that? You never did Army time, did you?" I nodded my head. "You did?" I nodded my head. "You went to Nam?" I raised my third finger straight into the air and smiled and he smiled back. "Atta boy" he said. "Well I was in charge of the liquor and cigarettes going over there—stuff with tax seals on 'em? Jesus, it was like working inside of a barrel of snakes. There was not a single—honest to you, now—not a single straight guy in on any of the deals I ran. Every single person there took. The generals, the warrant officers, the civilians who made the stuff or shipped it—hah! I'll tell you some time about the guys who run the trains in West Virginia! Hah!—and the guys over there: they were so bent, they had to use periscopes to comb their hair in the morning. The ones who had hair. Most of them were so slippery, they had Teflon heads. I kept telling my boss—tough black guy from Boston, the first black police captain they had there, *and* a lawyer: tough son of a bitch— I kept saying to him 'Harold, those crooks are the worst crooks in the world, and I can prove it.' And he would pour himself another drink of J. W. Dant 100 Proof which he drank from a Japanese cigarette tin, it used to hold Peace cigarettes, which is why he did it I guess, and he would say 'Abe, why

145

don't you do us all a favor and not know they're crooks? Because if you don't, if you ever do something dumb like send me a memo and keep carbons and make it official, a Complaint, then I'll have to buck it up, and the guys who *really* run Treasury, right? the guys who eventually, it ends up, own the stocks in the companies we're dealing with that are crooked, will be forced to cut their losses, run an investigation, fire their crooked middle-echelon people for being inefficient crooks, some tired Senator who needs publicity will run an Investigation, the TV cameras will be there, we'll both have to testify, our brave allies in Indochina will have to execute a hundred crooks who work for *them,* and some night, Rose and I will be at some lousy dinner with the Marines playing Muzak music for the President's lousy crab pancakes, and he'll come up to me—I swear I can smell the sweat off that guy across a room—and he'll say "Try not to fuck it up any more, will you, Harold? Once more and you'll be running a private phone-tapping company in Roxboro" and I'll have to simper and nigger him for just long enough to feel like I have to have you transferred to Alaska border surveillance liaison just to keep my ego floating.' Huh? Do you believe this? So mostly I kept my mouth shut. That's what you do in D.C."

Annie shook her head and I shook mine. It was like listening to a really bright physicist tell you how the winds in outer space weren't winds but really worked like winds just the same. I shook my head and said "So you cut out?"

He lit a cigarette and crossed his legs. The ankles were bare beneath his pants and he wore those city shoes, which were curling and pulpy now, battered, worn down. He said "Sort of."

After a while he asked us where we were from and what we did. I told him we were from New Hampshire and we were cutting out too, sort of, and then I stopped, and he knew enough to stop asking. I didn't, I didn't want to—I kept looking at the top of Annie's head—and I said "Do you practice law any more?"

146

"Not that kind."

Annie said "What kind, Abe?"

He sucked at the cigarette and the smoke came out with his words as if to hide them: "My kind."

"Oh" she said. "I'm sorry."

He said "What for?"

"I don't know" she said. "For asking. And because you have some things on your mind. Would you like another beer?"

He put the cigarette out and rubbed his chest. I could hear the wheeze of his lungs, I heard him work at breathing. His face was whiter, it was almost gray, and Annie moved as if to stand. I touched her to keep her there and we waited. He insisted on a deep breath and it came. He said "I smoke too much" and smiled his rueful sweet smile. Then he said "This place—" he waved his hands around—"this place: I could tell you about the oil refinery they're trying to put in up the coast from here, near the Naval station. Crooked? Washington, Maine, the whole world."

I went into the kitchen for the last three beers that were sitting on the last of the ice. I stayed there a while, looking out the window into the fog that hung between us and the boathouse over the long meadow. I popped the cans and brought them in and Annie was saying "—and maybe we'll take teaching jobs again or something. There are schools around here. The living's good. It's a good place to stay, don't you think?"

Abe said "Very good place. I wish I could stay."

She said "Where do you have to go?"

He lit a cigarette and drank some beer. "Circumstances, Miss Anne. I keep having these circumstances, and I keep having to leave. I keep hiding out and I keep leaving."

She said "Where?"

"I don't know. I thought I'd do a little Appalachian Trail walking. I don't know."

I said "It's pretty rugged around here. Your pack looked heavy."

He said "It's heavy."

147

She said "If you need some food and things—if you need to stay here, maybe we can help you." She looked at me. I waited. "If you need us to."

He looked at me too. I nodded but didn't speak. He said "Nah. Before I was married I used to walk in New England, I know my way around."

"Are you in pretty good condition?" she said.

He smiled that smile and said "Good enough."

She nodded to him and I watched them both. I said "We haven't told anyone you're here. We don't have a phone, we don't know anyone around here. Probably, you could stay a while."

He said "You two aren't crooks."

Annie said "You aren't either."

"Got to go back" he said. He put his cigarette out and stood. "Thank you for your time. And beer. The talk. Back to the old church, huh? I'll maybe see you soon, huh?"

Annie said "Whenever you want, Abe. Just come over."

I said "Sure" and she looked at me. I said "Whenever you want, Abe." She smiled, and he smiled at her, then looked at me as if he'd heard me say something else. He walked through the front parlor and into the kitchen and out, and we came behind him, to the edge of the fog at the door. He stepped into it and we couldn't see him.

Annie said "He's sad."

His voice came back from the pearly darkness: "Don't you worry, Miss Anne."

She looked at me—her face was young and frightened, I looked into it for what she had seen in his—and she called back "I won't, Abe. You take care and I will too." His silence came back. I locked the door.

It rained a heavy cold rain and we slept in late, huddling together under the old quilts and covers, waking slowly, gently rubbing our feet back and forth as we rose from sleep like amphibious creatures swimming ashore. There was no ice and Annie thought the eggs might be bad, and the bacon was brownish-green, so we made some coffee and powdered milk, ate dry cereal, did the dishes together, then lay around the house drinking more coffee, reading, saying little, doing nothing useful for a change. Annie went upstairs and came back with *Moby-Dick,* which I hadn't seen since last winter. I had the paper edition of *The Elements of Style*—"If one is to write, one must believe—in the truth and worth of the scrawl, in the ability of the reader to receive and decode the message"—but I couldn't believe in writing as a way of sending a message, unless you were sending a message to yourself; in which case, if you wanted to do it right, you better not be using codes at all: you better be stripping things to the bone. The only way to talk is straight. As Abe would have said: "Right? Huh? Am I telling you? *Straight."* So I put *Elements* down and drifted, looking for a book to settle in. I went through a couple of rooms, touching the tacky wood, smelling mildew and old moistnesses, looking at faded colors and darkened walls, hearing the old house creak and settle in the storm as if it were a ship. I came back to the kitchen where Annie was looking at pages and sipping instant coffee and said "Hey babe, read me some Melville."

"I can't read this book" she said.

"So what are you doing?"

"I'm skimming it."

"How can you skim *Moby-Dick?"*

She said "I keep skipping around until I find a fantastic passage and after it ends I get bored and then I look for something else good. That's how."

"I thought you didn't read novels any more."

"I'm not reading, I'm skimming."

"You know, you can make me happy in spite of yourself."

She said "Mm" and looked at the book and then, not looking up, said "Go back and work and have a good time and good-bye."

Which is why I'm here now, and happy. Annie's coming

back so fast, so surely—she's wiping the winter out, and I know she won't get away from what happened, she'd be a monster if she did, but she's getting through the worst of it. It wasn't losing two children. It wasn't that nonsense with Baker, I think. The poor sucker. The son of a bitch. It wasn't anything she did. It was living in herself those months, that was the worst, I think. I know it was the worst for me. Sometimes I forget I'm missing a thumb, but I can't get rid ever of a minute of those days and nights in New Hampshire. Maybe they'll turn into poems. It doesn't matter as much as I thought it might. If she stays here. If she stays, if she doesn't fall back into herself and get lost. But I think also I'm worried about Abe and I don't know why. It has to do with Annie, and I think I'm afraid she'll fall into him—whatever he is, whatever he'll do. She said it: I wanted her to come back to the world from herself and here he is, the world, and she's attracted to him somehow—not sexually, of course; in some deep sorrowful way—and now I don't feel sure I *want* her moving toward the world. Let's face it. I know it. I want her moving toward me, only me. I wonder if I'd rather have her nuts the way she was or healthy and in the outside world. And it isn't even that simple. I'm coming here more and more, or thinking about here more and more, and thinking more and more about writing it down in these notebooks. So I'm asking for her on *my* terms. I'm making her my book, if what I think, suspect or fear is true. I'm scared enough to try to own her with words. Which is something I thought I got over long ago.

Well, nobody ever promised you it was easy, friend. She's getting healthy. Take it as it comes. You and Annie are living *together*. That's so much. And still there's the boathouse, and the lantern throwing odd shapes, hissing, lighting the pages and the palimpsest of plans for the beautiful boat. If you could build a boat, where would you sail?

I'd stay here. I'd run electric wires in here and prop the place up, I'd electrify the house and put in lights and heat and a stove that didn't need so much attention, running water, make it a place where the life we lead needn't be a project. I'd get a job and we'd live here and do our work. Maybe we'd adopt a kid. Probably we wouldn't: we're too old together for that now, we'd be too scared, he'd intrude too much, we wouldn't love him right.

Yes we would.

There wouldn't be time to write poems.

Look at what you're writing now.

Well I *will* write poems.

Really?

No.

Really.

No.

So put your slicker on and go back to the house and tell her its time for her to put her boots and slicker on and go for a walk in the bogs and get down to the ocean and see what it's like in a storm.

And maybe I will write poems.

How much maybe?

Dammit, maybe pretty much.

Then stay here.

Yes. And look at the leather and metal on the walls, at the window frames that someone made, at the plans for the beautiful boat. Stay here. Don't stop living on your own a little bit. She never will.

No, she won't. And maybe she'll never come back all the way.

Well neither will you. Will you?

No.

Then probably there's hope.

More rain, more submarine days, drifting in small places like people inside a tiny boat, tightening muscles and growing wary in order not to bump one another, feel one another, have to contend. The air outside feels brown, like the sky in a tinted photograph you find in someone's attic. We don't have a real attic, we have a trap door in the bedroom ceiling; above it, there's the space beneath the roof, a million corpses of cluster flies, all sorts of larvae and scurrying long-tailed shimmery things, and no books, magazines, letters, documents —no clues. Writing this feels different. Reading this feels different. Something is changing, something is changing now. There's a membrane in the house, I sense it between us as we drift in the indoor fogs of long rainy days. We touch each other a little less—a little less frantically, maybe, so maybe we're just getting used to being married again—and we watch each other more. That is, Annie watches me more; I suppose I've always studied her, at least since we lost the babies. There's something *wary* in our house. It's made of both of us. It's us, we're giving something off, a kind of gas or mist, some subtle stink of fear we generate is making clouds in the house and they're drizzling watchfulness. We're sidling a little. We're looking for fright. So the air inside looks clouded, as if there's a membrane every place on the air and it's a little smeared. We're seeing things through dirty glass and we don't know why. Something like that—something like that is happening.

And at the end of a day, like now, hiding in here— why did I call it *hiding?*—with the lantern on, the insects gathered inside, the sky pressed down to nearly the earth, my papers and speckled books piled up beside me on an old milk-bottle box, my chair mildewing in the moisture, the fields outside alternately steaming mist and wincing under rain needles, I see us in brown-tinted pictures, hazy snapshots made in poor light or seen through weakening eyes:

Annie at sink. She leans against the deep enameled trough, her hand is on the rusted pump we don't use. She's turning as I walk into the kitchen, and we see her neck cords straining—just to turn around?—and see the beginning of a smile in the right-hand corner of her mouth, or maybe the death of a smile not started. Her big strong hands dominate the bottom of the picture. Her face (which also could be turning away) takes charge of the top.

Phil at kitchen door. Am I shaking off water like a shaggy dog? Am I making all that blurry motion as a camouflage inside of which I study her and study her, squint down her eyes and mouth like a doctor in search of disease? I could define her posture in a dozen ways, retell it so she's more than a dozen people, that's what my shape says. And now, studying my study of her, I could make myself twelve people too. One picture worth twenty-four lives: wrong, because the arithmetic of our hesitations doesn't account for twenty-five and twenty-six—the real people who stand there, looking at each other, for one clockless instant utterly confused. If there *are* real people in these pictures.

Annie in back parlor. She's lying in the dark room under a bright blue quilt. Her legs are drawn up, her arms are under her head, she stares at the ceiling—I see her eyes the way you see an animal's eyes in darkness: utterly the animal's, alien to you—and I have no idea what she feels. Then I think I do, and I think all the familiar subjects, and I think that I understand the spectrum of considerations that she floats in, alone. And then I think I don't. Most of the picture is impenetrable.

Annie varnishing the countertop. The smoothness of her strong arms, the smoothness of her strokes as she brushes on the polyurethane finish, the smoothness of its amber sheen on the wood she's sanded smooth. I watch her muscles move, the dipped concentration of her long neck, and she and what she does are utterly withheld from me.

Phil in the doorway. Holding with tight hands onto the molding at each side of the kitchen doorway, most of me in the front parlor, only my head leaning in. I see me from the front as I watch her. She isn't in the picture, but my face is so knotted and concerned, it could only be Annie I'm looking at. I can't make sense of my expression.

And a day like that, maybe days, looking and looking

at how the looking was done, puzzling at the moments, but feeling nothing specifically wrong and knowing that everything couldn't be right. Going back through the notebooks now, and looking for the plateau—that point in the geography of our days here where everything *was* right, and smooth, and untroublesome. Feeling decline and looking for the still moment before the ground tipped and things began to roll. And not finding it. Knowing it was there and not knowing, now, how to describe it. Things are getting away from us, from me—I'm not in control.

This is what Abe was talking about when he ate with us the other day. The three of us drank cheap Rioja and sucked spaghetti up, slurping our words around the food and laughing at Abe's jokes, Annie looking at his face throughout the meal, me studying Annie, watching in his expression the sadness and defeat she saw and which draws her. Abe saying "So he told me 'I don't give a shit about your hesitations, understand? I'm worrying about the goddam *case*.' Huh? So I told him 'Listen, pal, I may be a lawyer, and I may work for the government, but I'll be fucked—excuse me—if I actually go into court and *defend* this guy. He's a crook. He's a liar. He's a *lousy* crook. I could get six guys off Mulberry Street who could do his crookedness better than he does it. You know why,' I said, 'I'll tell you why: he's stupid. I'll be damned if I go into court for some stupid shmuck doesn't even know how to hire an architect who can draw up a PX that doesn't crumble when it rains!' And he tells me 'Fine. Don't go. I'll get you assignments so bad, you'll wish you were doing integration work for the President.' See, that was a big joke in Washington, because integration work for the White House was just about getting yourself a jackknife and whittling crosses for Southern congressmen to burn on people's lawns. And this guy's a *black!* He says 'I'm having bad feelings about you, Abe. I don't know what's wrong, but I think you're listening to the wrong people nowadays. Don't listen, Abe.' "

Annie said, twirling her spaghetti in a soupspoon, "What'd your family think, Abe?"

154

He looked at her as if he were going to apologize, or as if he hoped that she might tell him to forget the question. She waited, and he watched her wait. He poured more wine into my juice glass and motioned with the bottle at her, but she shook her head. He didn't pour more for himself. "Hell of a meal" he said. Then he said "My son was in a helicopter in Laos, where there isn't a war. He got shot by a machine gun some guy we counted as dead three times didn't shoot. He didn't die that month because we weren't having any casualties just then. So he didn't know about it."

"Oh shit."

He said "I hate to talk about him."

"Shit."

"Listen, Anne," he said, "don't be embarrassed. Phil. It's just so hard to talk about him for me."

I said "I'm so—"

Annie said "Shit."

I nodded and drank wine. Abe looked at the coiled spaghetti in its sauce. Annie closed her eyes—it was like watching someone leap into icy water—and she said "You told me your wife died?"

I looked at the wine in my glass. I heard Abe's breath go out. Then he said "She died."

We sat in the silence that ebbed steadily outward from the point of Annie's plunge. We sat, we listened, I couldn't look up. The rings of silence drifted out. Annie almost shouted "Tell us about Washington, Abe. Tell us something else."

He said "I don't know what to say."

She said "Anything?"

I heard his breath go in, I heard him draw it in again. He said "Well. All right, the President dribbles when he eats." Everyone laughed.

We've been having Abe Discussions: Who is he/I don't know. So how come you're so interested in him/Aren't you. Yeah but not the way you are/You make it sound like I'm having an affair with him. Come on you know I don't mean that/That's what you make it sound like. But you know I don't mean that/But that's how you make it sound. But how come the old guy fascinates you so much/I don't know I don't know he's so sad. But there's plenty more than that/We have something in common. What/I don't know. But it's something boy/Yes it is.

We've been having those. And we've been getting angrier, we're spending more time not having picnics, not driving around, not talking very long, very easily. The rain stays with us. Even if the day starts hot and clear, there's mist on the back hills and it clouds up soon enough and by the afternoon we're pinned inside. Some afternoons on the soft wood floors of a barn, I play myself at mumblety-peg, dropping the knife, dividing the squared-off playing area into squares and triangles, scratching my initial into every part I win from me, or lose to me, dropping the knife and watching it stand blade down in whatever area's left. Some afternoons I shuffle gear around in the barns. I don't want to throw anything away, there's something awesome in the old leather and weathered scrap wood, so I stack things in different places, then later move the stacks, but everything stays. Annie does more sketching, or she lies on the day bed and she doesn't read. Sometimes she puts her slicker on and goes up the hill to the church and talks to Abe. When she comes back she doesn't tell me what they've said. If I ask her she hides inside, and all I see is the person I live with. She wants what he's carrying, or it wants her, and I don't know what to say. I don't know how to say what I don't know. It feels like the winter in New Hampshire. Something is beginning again. I'm hanging on.

Today I took a pry bar and a heavy mallet and went upstairs to the small room that overlooks the back field. The room needed doing, but I didn't have to do it today. We were drifting downstairs, not touching, and I felt that winter coming on again and I got scared. The first thought was to get out to the boathouse and write down *Here it comes,* but I knew I wouldn't have anything to write down after that. Something he carries from the world. That's what I mean: writing things like *Something he carries from the world.* Like I'm talking in code to myself. Stuttering out how frightened I've become. All these jagged sentences I'm making when—I look through the early notebook—I was supposed "to organize, pull it into lines, directions." Well, the lines of narrative are getting tangled, friends. Friends, we are getting tangled in the lines.

I wonder if I'm doing any good, now that the narrative's stopping. I don't know. But I don't know what else to do. So I keep the pen moving and make believe the motion's smooth and say I went upstairs with the pry bar and silver-headed mallet. I had an ancient mildewed sheet which I nailed above the door inside, then I wet it down with a pitcher of water from the kitchen. I shut the bedroom door, made sure the sheet was clinging to the door, opened the window and looked through the rain at the boathouse where I am now. Then, with the boat knife, I slit the wallpaper—cracked, bulging, split so that it looked like a map—along the seam between the walls and ceiling. I lifted the mallet and closed my eyes and swung it into the wall. Plaster rattled inside the wall and fell. It sounded like rats running. I swung again, and chunks popped out through the ancient painted paper into the room. The heavy dust hung like water vapor. I stuck the straight end of the pry bar in and pulled, and then I turned it and, with the curved end, pulled harder, and soon I was tearing great hunks of wall down onto myself. I worked from left to right, from bottom to top, and I seized and gouged, yanked at the house we'd holed up in, and it didn't take long for me to be covered with heavy sweat and the sandy particles of plaster. The hair on my arms was white, and my chest was covered with whiteness the sweat cemented on.

It looked as if the room had been shelled. The long wall opposite the window was stripped, and little pieces of wallpaper from the ceiling which the pry bar had pulled hung down like puckers of wound. The wall itself was nothing now but lath running horizontally, like long-running bones, like ribs; the whole wall grinned at me. The lath, nailed at five-foot intervals to vertical two-by-fours, was light brown, shaggy, and in places I could see where the dry rot had gotten it. I could push through the wood with my fingers. But I didn't go downstairs to the barn for extra lath to rebuild. Later I'd rebuild if I had to. Now I was breaking. I went to work on the short wall, gouging, pulling, tearing the house down onto myself, and that took no time at all. And then I was hauling at the other long wall, the one with the window that looked out over the blue-green grass, the mists that steamed up, the silver-bleached boathouse that leaned as if it might fall. I looked at it as I swung and, ripping beneath the windowsill, I staggered, straightened, and brought the end of the pry bar through the glass. It exploded in at me as if the winds had all come down. I stood in front of the broken window, dust in the air as if the air were dust, the shattered walls in chunks and gobbets on the floor. I didn't know what I had done. I didn't know what I was going to do.

I heard a hiss of breath and looked to the door. Arms and a face were pressed at the sheet and it jumped, floated at me, tore from the nails above the door and came in. I closed my eyes and sat down. I leaned against the wall near the window, sitting in the glass and debris, opened my eyes and watched her peel the sheet from her body and face, saying "What the fuck are you *do*ing?"

"You won't believe what I thought you were. What you looked like."

"What?"

"Never mind. Never mind."

"What's all this, Phil?"

"You know what this is. It's pulling down plaster preparatory to the husband putting plaster board up so there are new smooth walls in the room."

"It sounded like you were tearing the house apart."

158

"I was."

She sat against the opposite walls, the house's brown ribs, plaster still stuck between them in gray crumbling fragments. She watched me and it looked familiar—the kind of slit-eyed watching I've been doing so much of—and she said "You look like a ghost."

I looked at the rubble between us and nodded.

After a while she said "It's awful goddam hot in here, Phil."

I nodded at the floor.

"Are you okay?"

I said "Sure, babe."

"You look pretty bad. You know?"

I looked at her, the long lean legs in shorts, the oversize tee shirt, her hair in two braids, the look on her face of a small child's confusion.

"Annie, I love you."

"I accept" she said. Her big mouth smiled a small child's grin—she looked almost shy—and she said "So why don't you tell me what's wrong. As long as you love me."

I said "Look—" and her smile went away, her face seemed to mimic my voice, respond to it in advance, because she really knew.

We were quiet for a while and then she said "Abe?"

I didn't look up when I said "Yup."

"Well he bothers me too" she said.

"I mean he's a nice enough guy. He's funny as hell."

"And he's sad."

"Well that's the part I mean" I said. "He makes you sad."

"Boy, doesn't he."

"Honey, you keep *chasing* it, you keep going after the sadness. Whatever it is he has. Christ, he wears it like shaving lotion, I can *smell* it coming off him."

She pulled her knees up and her feet in sneakers scraped through the pieces of house. She folded her hands in front of her knees and held herself tight. She looked at her hands and

159

said "I know, and I don't know what it is either, Phil. I'm not acting crazy on purpose."

"You're not acting crazy. I'm acting scared."

She looked up when she said "I think I'm acting crazy a little."

"Nah."

She looked at me as if I were going to give her an important permission, or forgiveness, or tell her that she wasn't, after all, very ill.

So I said "Nope. No. I just wonder about him. What the hell. If he interests you, go see him. I mean, he is a nice guy."

"You're saying that as a favor."

"I don't do you favors."

"Because you don't want me to be scared."

I watched her, huddled against the wreckage of the house, and I said "You're scared already. I think I am too."

She said "That's right."

I said "That's right."

"So what do we do? I mean, what the hell *is* he?"

I said "We're going to find out, babe. We'll wait and it'll happen and then we'll see."

She said "You know I'm not leaving you. The way—"

"If you talk while the men are working you'll be asked to leave."

"No, Phil—"

"Shh."

Which didn't solve anything, of course, and she went downstairs after a while and I pulled more wall down. And I went to bed tonight, after she was asleep, curled naked under a sheet like a baby, like the witch I live with, small in the big wooden bed we've carried from house to house to house. I took my clothes off and lay beside her and itched and tried not to thrash. I turned over and stuck my head into the pillow and reached above it to knock three times for luck on the wooden headboard. I sat up. I didn't know until then that I'd been knocking for luck on the headboard every night we'd slept in Maine. I carried my clothes downstairs and dressed in the kitchen and came out here, lit the lantern, opened the book. I'm sitting here asking myself what I knew that made me fear my sleep, or what in my sleep I came to know. I'm writing this in the boathouse, asking, and I don't know what to reply.

A nnie went shopping—the fourth time she'd gone by herself—and I went back upstairs to finish cleaning the walls of the extra bedroom. All the walls lay on the floor. The window was shattered in the midst of wooden stripes. The air was fogged, still, from the day before. With a heavy putty knife, I scraped the surface of the lath, pushing at the plaster in between the stripes of lath so it would fall into the wall now instead of falling in between the lath and the wallboard when I hammered the new gypsum sheets up; chunks of plaster would bulge the new board, and the board would break from the stress of covering something round when it was laid on flat. Shoving the plaster pieces through was easy, all it took was time. I listened on the transistor radio to *Camelot,* and the listening was harder than the work. But scraping the surface of the lath was nasty, because the dust rose up in my nose and hung in the air for my eyes to blink in, for my throat to swallow, I was working in a storm of broken house, gagging, weeping, sneezing as if I were allergic either to the work or the house itself. And plaster pieces went falling in, scurrying down like rats between the walls, and I scraped and jammed, scraped and jammed, and above it all—a big-chested baby with an evil lilt—Richard Burton sang songs of innocence and betrayal about a place where the weather was always what men needed it to be. I scraped a wide long swath across the lath strips and the putty knife snapped where the blade went into the handle; it sang a metal tone, then skipped across the wall and

161

buried itself in the rubble of paper and wallboard. I screamed *"Fuck!"* as Burton mumbled "–ot" and Annie came in.

I shouted "Pull the goddam sheet across or the dust gets into the house!"

She stood as she had the day before: swathed by the hanging sheet, a child's conception of a ghost.

I said "Get away from the sheet and pull it back across, Annie."

She came all the way in, shut the door, put the sheet away from her and across in front of the doorway, and looked at me. "You look terrible."

"Thank you."

"God. Let's get out of here, Phil. Hey, we're going to dinner."

"Splendid. I didn't know the governor was back. When's his car coming?"

"Phil, you have times when you're really delightful, you know? This is one time like that. You're really a pleasure."

"Thank you."

"And you look terrible."

"Thank you."

"And we're dining–uh. With Abe." She shut the radio off and backed up to the sheet.

I put my fingers on the lath and ran them down. I said "You might not believe this, but I actually don't quite understand."

"Well, he asked me to shop for him and I did–he gave me the money–and–God, he wanted a lot of whisky, all kinds of things–and we're supposed to go over there about five o'clock for drinks and he's making us dinner."

"How did you know he wanted you to shop for him? Did he come over?"

"Fuck you, Sorenson. I went over and you know it and so what."

"Yeah. Fuck me. Okay, you went over."

"So?"

162

"Nothing."

"Yeah. Nothing. So?"

"So nothing. Except—I mean you can go wherever you want to—except, I mean how come he couldn't go into town by himself?"

"No car?"

"How about going in with you."

"Phil, you really turn me off when you get clever with me, you know that?"

"Yup."

"Yup. Christ. You *know* he's hiding. *I* know he's hiding. He's running away or something, I don't know. We both know it. So why teach it to me? I am prepared to confess"—she spread her arms in front of the sheet and looked at the sagging ceiling in its smoke of plaster dust—"that Abe is a ferocious criminal and he's on the run. Who isn't?"

I walked across the ruins of the room and bent over as her chin went up higher and kissed her at each nipple once. I said "Who isn't. Would you let me make you a pot of coffee?"

She put her forearm behind my neck and locked my head there. She said "You drink it with me."

"Yup."

"And keep your mouth shut."

I nibbled and kept my mouth shut. And of course we went that afternoon—across our yard past the sweet well and up the hill that was yellow with buttercups, white with daisies, up on through the blueberry bog that turned our shoes purple and to the church. Insects sang, a cowbird faked pain, the winds coming up from the sea were soft and salty and carrying pine smells from the forest between us and the ocean. The light was on in the top of the squat church. And upstairs, past the abandoned chairs and scattered hymnals, past the old dust and darkness, in the far corner of the hot still second story, surrounded by stale air, there was Abe.

I noticed first that his fine white feet were bare, luminescent (like the skin of deep-water fish) when he went from the

163

light's core of brightness that we sat around. The nails were trimmed short, as a walker's should be, and his black cuffs were rolled up once. He wore no belt, and instead of a shirt he wore an underwear vest; I saw blue veins on his sagging white chest, the tufted hair turned white, the lack of muscle where the armpits began. His elbows were sharp because his muscles in the arms were slack, and his chest slumped too far in, his stomach too far out, for him to be as young as he suggested by his bearing, or for him to have walked as far and carried as much as he said. His soft feet curled at the floor and his body expanded in the air as I watched him move, and it felt as if he were showing us—the man from Washington whose government revealed its policies to other nations by means as subtle as the placement of prepositions in public announcements—that his time was drained more nearly to the bottom than his laugh, his cigarette smoke or his long tasty stories would show.

The light came from an electric lantern and a kerosene lamp that he'd mounted on a stack of old hymnals. The lantern pointed at the ceiling and lighted it, and the kerosene lamp spread lateral light. The oily light of the lamp didn't carry far, and we sat in small yellowness, as if we were painted on parchment; the electric light that went straight up was a tight fine brightness, and it made a circle of brilliance overhead, like an opening in a cave. Around us was the darkness, and then the light we sat within. It seemed as if there were no walls, no ceiling, as if we weren't in a church or even building: someone was dreaming us, setting us out on a stage. (As I write this I'm struck with the guilt that lights my boathouse now; I make us more of words than events. Do I draw us by these lines into saneness?)

So we sat—I cannot answer my questions, all I can do is haunt myself—and Abe went in and out of the light. He had the Primus stove going, he said, somewhere in the darkness, and he was stewing a chicken with wine and bay leaves and tarragon, salt and pepper, and we would eat from plates that

164

Annie had brought up before. She sat across the light from me and I couldn't see her face. She was invisible in the brilliant light. And Abe walked in and out of darkness. He brought us Irish whisky in tumblers that Annie had brought, and we drank; the whisky was redolent of peat, it felt like smoke, and we drank more, and I sweated in the light or darkness—I couldn't tell the difference soon—and we talked. Abe told us about Washington and the government and the war in Vietnam, and Annie told him about New Hampshire—only geography, the seasons, temperatures and landscapes, not what New Hampshire really had been. And I kept seeing us—or do I only see us now?—as a series of shadows and brilliances, an etching on the dark.

Annie drank very quickly, I could tell by Abe's rapid movement to and from the other side of the light, the music of glass. But we all drank a lot, and I got hotter, the light and liquor made me sleepy and scared, I couldn't see enough, and soon I couldn't hear enough, and I kept talking and Annie murmured like rivers. I thought of the mill race behind the house in New Hampshire and I wanted to cry. I wanted to go back, and not be stupid with machines, and not lose the finger, not think of that pain, the absolute final clean pain that went beyond hurting into something lopped from the brain, the pure loss of it. Because that was Annie's loss to me: the severing of my flesh. That was when the baby fell out of her, who might have saved Annie the fight for her life.

So then I did cry. I heard the silence which meant that Abe had stopped talking. Listening into it, slitting my eyes at the light, I heard the *hush* of the Primus stove and our bubbling dinner, the soft drag of Abe's feet on the old floor. I closed my eyes and heard what he'd said before the silence: "Herself." I listened deeper, leaned my head at the air to hear harder and heard "She killed herself." I heard "Why do the mothers have to die?"

I said "What?"

Abe said "What?"

165

"Didn't someone say something, the mothers—what?"

Annie's voice was low, falling into the monotone I had heard in New Hampshire the length of a winter, the winter's fiercest wind: "He said his wife killed herself."

"Abe? *Who?*"

"My wife. Her name used to be Dora. She was fifty-six."

"Dora?"

"My wife. She killed herself."

I said "Was it your fault?"

Annie said "Shut up!"

I said "Christ, Annie, what the hell do you know. This is husbands talking. Right, Abe? When the wife kills herself, the husbands have to say that. Because—"

"Of course" Abe said.

Annie said *"Why?"*

He said "I don't know."

I smiled and nodded my head. The motion made me sick and I held still, but I smiled, because I knew what he meant, whatever he meant. The husbands always ask.

He said "Our son's name used to be Richie. The boy who got shot down. We didn't get his body back. We got this fat sergeant from Maryland, he talked like he was selling us death. Which is a promising career, and I couldn't blame him for practicing."

He poured more whisky for me and I drank it. He poured me more. I said "Thank you, Abe. This makes it easier."

"It always does" he said. "Then it doesn't."

"No," I said, "I mean the information. I'm sorry, but it does. Because I didn't know what Annie was doing here all the time."

"I didn't tell her."

"She knew" I said. "She would know. She would smell it. She would come up here and smell it. Like she was going to a library for information. She would come up here and do research on herself. Right?"

He said "You're asking me?"

166

"Her, you, anyone, it doesn't matter. Because that's what she was doing. So now I know."

Annie said "I'm glad it pleases you."

"It doesn't please me" I said.

"You sound like it pleases you."

Abe said "We aim to please."

"Abe," I said, "I'm sorry. This is a very nice dinner and I'm sorry everybody died."

"My wife didn't die. She killed herself. She walked into a car."

Annie said "They think maybe she wasn't trying—"

"She had to climb up an embankment near the house, walk down an exit ramp, hide near the road divider, wait for a fast car to come off the arterial—at three o'clock in the morning—and jump onto the window. She worked at it. Because she jumped so high she hit the windshield. She broke it with her face. Everyone was killed."

I heard Annie breathing through her fingers. I couldn't see her but I knew what she looked like. I rubbed my stump against my face.

Abe said "She broke it with her face."

It was quiet, then, except for the little stove and the bubble of food, the sound of Annie's breathing on her own skin. Abe moved about a little, then stood still. The light poured up to wherever it went—the ceiling, the sky, the top of the page; it wobbled out sideways and then stopped dead. Annie was invisible in glare, and Abe in darkness, I was already in the boathouse writing it down because I didn't know what to do in the top of the church, hating my need to be away to make it make sense.

"Her face" Abe said.

I said "Your only child?"

"Nah. There's a sweet daughter in Virginia with a husband who is such a shit, he wears toilet paper to work. He's a lawyer too. He's honest and he works hard and he's got the emotions of an ant. She's better. She's a termite. If you're collecting termites, you can have her. Well. Maybe not that bad. Maybe."

I said "Annie, you knew all this?"

"Pretty much."

"That's why, in the house—"

"Yeah. I wasn't doing my best."

"No. No. But you didn't want me to know, huh?"

"I didn't know what to tell you. It was Abe's, it wasn't ours."

"But he told you."

"That was different. We were—sharing."

"You were sharing."

"I'm sorry."

"You weren't sharing with me."

"Well I guess I wasn't, Phil."

"But you were telling him all about us?"

"Not all about."

"Some about?"

"Some."

Abe said "I'm sorry."

I said "Abe, could I ask you—were you fucking my wife?"

He sighed, he said "You know, I wish I was. I couldn't get it up for the American flag on Independence Day. Is that all right to say, Annie?"

She said "For you. Not him."

I said "I'm sorry. But you were, you know. You were getting more than I was. What I wanted to get."

Annie said "Tough tits, old boy."

I said "So you two were hanging around up here, smoking each other's skin and discussing your deaths. Well, I'm glad you found each other."

Abe said "She saved my life."

"I'm glad" I said. "Come on, Annie, let's go." I tried to stand up, then I tried again, then I drank more whisky and he shuffled over and poured me more. I said "How come you can see what I'm doing and I can't see you?"

168

Annie said "You know, you're so weak, Phil."

Abe said "It's his turn."

There was that steaming sound of silence again and she said "Right."

I said "What the fuck is *that?*"

Abe said "Right?"

Annie said "Right."

I said "Annie, what did he *tell* you? What was it up here? Babe?"

Abe said "I told her my wife did that. When I was still alive. She didn't love me enough to kill me first is what I told her. She ran away from me. Or something. Some place. Whatever she had on her mind, wherever she wanted to go, she wasn't planning on me. That's what I said. I was *some* kind of connection. But it was her son, see. She loved him more. One night she dreamed about a girl she never saw after college, she told me. And this girl said 'Have more babies' and she woke up, she couldn't stop crying. I kept saying 'What? What?' and all she told me was the dream. Have more babies. See? Because that was all that was left. Me. Us. A lousy world run by technicians with fifth-rate imaginations. A giant hospital. Her and me getting old with worse breath every morning and no more babies for her to have and us to take care of and try to keep from growing up and moving into a different time zone." He poured more liquor for himself this time, I heard his glass bang and bang again. "Have more babies. Sure. Because after that stopped she was living on her own. With me on her own. No more promises. No more hopes. Babies is hope, Phil. Surprises. You know what's coming, but with babies you never believe it. I used to get tears in my eyes at night when I saw Richie or Carol—she's the termite now—in their cribs at night. You know why? Because they'd grow up and leave us behind. But I used to not cry in the morning when we'd get them dressed. Because it was possible. Something was possible. And it wasn't just us, which is the hardest part of marrying someone —all that concentrated *us.* Anything could have happened. And maybe if they had just grown up, just gone away and despised us, huh? Except with Richie we had the ghost. And the ghost was—now you're on your own. That was the ghost: now you're on your own together, live without promises, don't have hopes, live what your life really *is*. That was the ghost that chased her onto the arterial at three in the morning and made her smash her face in the poor bastard's car window and leave me. Fucking bitch, Dora! *You ran out!"*

I heard Annie crying into her fingers. I was crying too. The three of us: a wake. We mourned for Abe in his undershirt, and the boy who died in Indochina, and the wife in a jelly on the windshield, and Annie, and me, two droolings of baby's body from between her legs, and my thumb in the high grass in New Hampshire, and England lost, and the new world we lost every day.

After a long time, after the soft cushings of his feet back and forth in the darkness, and after he hadn't moved for a while, with just the hissing of the Primus stove, Abe said "I think dinner's ready now." Annie giggled and stopped, then giggled more, and I laughed. I couldn't stop. Abe tried to talk, but he was laughing too hard. We all went on like that, and I was lying on my back, gasping, and then he whooped and we started again and couldn't end it, Annie gagging because she screamed and laughed at the same time. When we were simply panting, too tired and crazy to laugh any more, Abe groaned, and there was the soft sound of him rolling over on the floor. Then it was really silent in the bright bubble of light. We all lay still as if we were stuffed with our meal.

I t was a poisoned day, and we were down at the sea being sick. We had wakened late, and Annie had vomited a breast of stewed chicken and a bucket of whisky and wine. We'd both drunk Alka-Seltzers, stuffed aspirins down, and had lurched in bathing suits and sneakers, carrying blankets and

170

towels and a couple of bottles of beer, down around behind the house, down the long tangly field and into the pine forest where, a few days before, I'd buried the tombstones. It was a sour day. The sky was yellow, the clouds smeared like fat on a wide bright glass—I thought of Abe, of his wife smeared into a windshield—and the light that came through the clouds was blinding as the light we'd been suspended in upstairs in the church. The clouds and sky were blended: everything in the air was a barrier to seeing. The ground was wet, the high grass and devil's-paintbrush tangled on our legs, the pine trees bent low in our faces and scratched, there were gnat clouds and bug swarms of every itching high-whine variety; it was a day to be miserable in, and the sweat ran down us and we groused at the world in our breath-blowings, free-handed swattings, exclamations when the gnats went up our noses, pantings at the heat and stumblings through the rotted floor and painful prickly brush of the pine forest over the sea. We pushed up the hill without talking to one another, partly because we were winded and headached, sick with last night's liquor and revelation, partly because we hadn't known what to say from the time we woke. And then we made it up the hill and stood in the winds and then went down its steep eroded sea-face, more rock than dirt, more barrier or last resort than hill. There was only the one way to go, the way the little boats had once been hauled, because every place else on the cliff went down in a nearly straight line to the sea. It was below us, the coastal rocks were wet as old stumpy teeth in an ancient mouth, and the terns and gulls cried long distress, the sea rolled over the world at us and away, through the yellow haze, in smoke, because it was foggy the embers burned on the radio towers, warning all the ocean and earth to keep their distance from this place.

We climbed—we didn't hold each other's hands—to the flat rock we'd used before, and without talking we settled the blanket, pried our sneakers off, opened beer, sank like survivors of a sea wreck onto the stone. The air smelled of fish-

171

eries out of sight across the bay and around a half mile bend
of black stone beach, it smelled of kelp and gullshit, the sweat
of our drunk perspiration, the glue of our mouths, the pine
above us, the salt swells below. Everything danced at us in
the yellow glare and distances weren't true. The sound of the
sea rolls was the only regularity, the ticking of the only machine
that morning which worked.

Annie said "I'm thirsty but I can't drink this." It sounded
as if her throat were closing, furring up with growths. "The
smell—"

"It'll make you feel better, babe."

"Do I sound like you?"

"What do I sound like?"

"Nothing alive."

"Yup."

"Oh God. God, what a terrible night, Phil."

"The saddest man I know."

"He got so *drunk.*"

"I doubt he ever can get drunk enough."

"That's what he said."

"When you went to see him those times?"

"Did you really mind? Yes you did."

I said "I did. I couldn't help it. I understand he needed
you—"

"Yeah, well I needed him."

"Babe, for *what?* What's he got for you except dying?"

"Well—"

"Fuck that, Anne. I don't need that. Neither do you."

"How interesting."

"I'm sorry."

"No, you're probably right. Except, I *did* feel like I needed
him. Something he had."

"He doesn't look like your father."

"Thank you, Herr Freud."

"So what *is* it?"

"Someone else."

172

"What?"

"Someone else. Period. Finished. Over and done, no more talking about Abe." She said "Okay?"

I lay down and put my beer can next to my waist, drummed my fingers on its top and closed my eyes. I thought of myself down here, this night, some other night, fighting off moths and squinting into the lantern and writing with my bright blue ink about what she said—"Someone else"—and making it offer sense, yanking it into a shape I could cup and hold before me, rotate slowly, understand. I'm here and hardly understanding. But up there, instead of working on her words, I drummed on the beer can and only felt. And medicine is more than counting the pulse.

I said "You know, I haven't written poem one. Well, poem one. I've got maybe a couple of whole ones."

"Are they bad?"

"Incredibly."

"Have you seen my sketches?"

"No."

"They're worse."

I sat up, but my head rang like bells and I lay down again. "When you say that, do you mean you've looked? In the boathouse—at what I've been writing?"

She said "Easy, boy."

"You haven't, have you?"

"Wow. Thank you. No."

"I'm sorry."

"Yeah."

"Come on, babe."

"Of course."

"Goddam it, Anne, don't *do* that."

"Well how do you expect me to sound? Gosh, Phil, it sure is lovely that you think I'm a thief. Sneak. Peeper? What would you call the crime you have in mind?"

"Annie: I apologize, and I'll show you some time what I'm doing. Okay?"

"No."

"Thank you."

"Thank *you.*"

After a while I said "Annie?"

"Watch it, boy."

"Hon?"

She blew her breath out, and I heard her smile. She said "I can *hear* how careful you're being."

I chuckled so she could tell that she was right; when I did, I didn't bend my lips. I said "How come he's hiding?"

"His daughter. But I thought we weren't talking about Abe."

"Well. He's hiding from the ant?"

"Termite. Yeah: he's running away from his own child. She wants him to live with her."

"Wouldn't it be easier just to say no?"

"Apparently she doesn't understand that."

"It sounds more like his wife. The way she couldn't—this is according to *him*—the way she couldn't stay with only him. Without the son. It sounds like he can't stay with only her. Without whatshername, Dora. Without her."

I heard her try not to let her breath hiss out. But I heard it hiss. She said very evenly, "I'll bet. I'll bet you're right."

And then I said very evenly "Sort of like you, huh?"

She said "Excuse me?"

"Like you without your sons and/or daughters—I keep thinking sons, don't you? Like you without our kids."

"Oh."

"You know what I mean?"

She said "I guess he's on the run all right."

"Sort of like you."

I banged my stump against the top of the can. She said "Phil?"

I said "There's no one home."

174

Now, in August, when the mist at night hangs in the valleys and at morning makes the air feel moist as the insides of a cloud, the spiders are building their webs. All summer they've made them, and we've walked through the forest with web on our faces, watched the big yellow-and-black ones which we think are poisonous weave great diamond shapes across the wilting chokecherry, brushed from one another's clothes the early morning webs which, soaked with dew, shine on us in the sun as if we'd grown bright scales. But now, in August, they're all in earnest; they work as if the summer webs were accidental, *this* is on purpose and part of a serious scheme. They hang in webs from the eaves of the house, across the doors, on the insides of windows which we haven't moved for a day. Coming up a hill we see them pendant on trees and they fill the horizon underneath the low wiry branches of pine. Their webs in the morning glitter, and at night they catch the yellower lights of the living room and kitchen. They're every place with us. Every web's inhabited, every spider is still: the wind blows the webs on the roof of the outhouse like sails on a ship and the spiders don't move, like sailors they hang on. The world is filled with creatures hanging on. The world is windy, and I think she could blow loose.

I think of her and Abe. I think of Abe, imagine him with his wife, his son. I see him without them. I think of his daughter, the insect, and I see him without her. He is here without them, but I think of Abe with his kin, and they blow away. I rub my hands on these pages as if I can coax up lives and start again to fill the background in.

QUESTIONS:

What was Abe's daily life like? Where did he sleep? Did he and his wife still make love before she killed herself? *This is important:* did they do the middle-aged screw? What did he eat for breakfast? Did *he* dribble food like the President? How did he get to work? In which Federal office building did he practice the government's law?

Did Abe really love his son as much as he says? The

answer is probably *Yes*. But he's hardly stated it out in clear sharp prose for the rest of us to understand. What proportions are his guilt? Did he work for the government that killed his son? *Yes*. Does he really feel responsible? *I think yes*. Is that why he ran away?

What *are* his motivations? Why is he here? Why so ill prepared, yet outfitted? What does that tell us about his character? Is he on his way to his death? Is he running away from the idea of what he's been part of? Is that why he's come to the coast? None of these questions are answered for us.

What about the daughter he says he hates? How much can parents hate their kids? Does she smother him? Remind him of his wife? Why did he really flee her?

Is she like Annie? Is that why he likes my Annie so much? And does she think of him the way she thinks of her father? Is that why she's attracted to him? What do these possibilities tell us about their characters?

Does he do the middle-aged screw with my wife? Is she his final hold on the world? Is he her *memento mori?* Can I imagine them rolling on his sleeping bag, her holding him in because he wilts? Does she go down on him as an act of contrition to her past and his presence and what he's endured and what she's fled? Are there implications here? Does this help us to understand his character? Hers?

Why can't I know more about him?

What does this failure reveal to us about my character?

If I am making narrative here, setting down what happens so that Annie and I can be sane, why isn't there more to set down? Abe keeps ending up as *here*. That's all. *Right*. There's no information we can use. We're in the dark. We don't know why they're acting as they do. *Right*. They keep behaving like irrational people, and in narrative I ought to be able to make them act like people I can comprehend.

Have you ever considered that you're making them into characters you *say* are acting like people? *Yes*.

And what's the difference?

176

None. *Right.* Really?
How should *I* know? All I do is write it down.
Why did you start that out about the webs?
Aren't they every place?
Yes, but why now? Why do you write them now?
Don't you know what spider webs in August mean?
How should I know? All I do is live here.
Don't you really know?
Do I have to?
Don't you want to?
Yes. The webs tell us autumn is coming. Things are beginning to end.

I will not write again—not to speak to myself, not for the sake of what I need to think I know, and not for the sake of what I've called saneness, not for Annie, not for what I've said she is or known she is or wished her to be. This is the end. The boathouse pitches with the dreams of its palimpsest, the lines of the drawing glow on the moldering wood. Insects fog the air like a fine live mist, and the darkness outside is the ocean's. I smell the blood in my nose and hear its rhythms in my skull as if I sniffed the sea salt and listened, listened, waiting for surf to beat on the New World's rocks. I stood on the cliff above the rocks, a hill away from where I'd buried the tombstone wafers, and I looked at the body below. I sat in here and looked at the corpses of my words—the accidental deaths of my intentions, my visions, perceptions and hopes—and I saw how never had I made in fine straight shapes what really happened in our days and nights at this our final harbor. The words—my needs—polluted my will to keep us sane by saying what had been and what was being. I have not told the truth. I will not lie again, not this way. No more lousy poems, no more still-born narratives: I'll do whatever I do, and then it will be done, and I'll be through. And then I'll try to sleep, and then wake up. In a minute I'll stop this talking. In a minute I'll stop.

This is where I was. I was looking at what I have said these weeks, and thinking that I simply hadn't the en-

177

ergy to tell these pages—myself—of our days since Abe in his abandoned church had served himself to us in the cone of light in its shell of utter dark. I didn't want to talk about the work on the roof, the painting of sills, the fastening of shiny hinges to doors, our silences, our speech, the touch-and-go of our life, holding on and letting go—we were a tide of need and heedlessness—until we were fearful and crazy beyond the reach of words and projects, able only to fuck in a frenzy and slide away into sleep with a hope that in the morning we would stop and think, and then, in the morning, finding no time for anything but standing-still panic and a flight into solitary chores. So I was here, and not understanding what I'd written. I was doing that, and wishing for help, and Annie walked in like a ballerina—not graceful, but every muscle clearly under control, her body trembling with the effort to be calm. She said "I'm sorry. I don't want to disturb you—"

"No, that's all right, babe. Nothing good is happening here. You're rescuing me. What's up?"

"Abe."

"What else?"

"Phil, he's drunk out of his mind. He's running around naked in the woods."

"And scaring the hell out of you."

"He's running around without anything on. Whimpering. He wouldn't talk to me. Or stop. Anything. He's sort of dragging through the woods getting all scratched up. He ran past the house, I was out there on the steps drinking coffee and he ran past me—"

"Because he wanted you to see him?"

"I don't know."

"Sure."

"Well he sure didn't stop when I did see. When I called him. God. Phil, he's crazy. He's filled with—I don't know: he's crazy, Phil." She was standing absolutely still, tall and trembling and controlled, like a dancer locked on her toes. Her face was wet and red and I didn't know what to tell her. She said "Phil? Can you come?"

178

So of course I did. We took the lantern from the boathouse and walked—she was leading me, she carried no light; I came behind with the lantern, as if to light the way for whoever was following me—and we went back around to the front of the house, through the high damp grass and chattering insects, in the mist that made the moon a high dim blur. We passed the steps, where her coffee cup lay propped on its handle. I turned there, and saw the light in the top of the church, the ghost she'd seen for days which I had denied. I turned again, and saw her legs, luminescent, going around once more to the back of the house and, holding my useless light, I followed her. I always followed her, didn't I? And he wasn't there, but his trail was—grass whipped aside as if an animal had dragged—and she in the darkness knew to follow the beaten weeds and I followed her. We went down the meadow, she ahead and panting, I breathing to her tune, and then we loped the shallower stretch, and then slowed down at the edge of the wet black silence of the pine trees where I'd buried the stones. We walked on top of their grave. I smelled the sea, the rotting needles, heard the ocean over the hill before us, heard the animals diving away in the brush. Annie ran on, but I walked, and soon she was over the hill, the sound of her panting gone, the shush and rustle of the tide now louder than her frightened breathing or the whistle of pines in the salt wind.

Because I thought I knew what I'd find. I saw myself standing at the top of the hill above the rocks and the beating water, looking down. And instead of hurrying, I slowed. I was my own nightmare, my thighs were knotted and heavy, I heard a thin high dragging whistle and, in my waked and underwater dream, I blew the tune of *Frère Jacques, Frère Jacques, dormez-vous? dormez-vous?* and I could stop that stupidity no more than I could speed my pace. Because I knew what I would find.

And when I reached the top, and the wind plugged back my screeching song between my lips, and I saw in the mist those high burning embers, I stopped and went to my knees and closed my eyes. Like a monument to voyagers, she stood at the edge of the rocks that went down to the sea. I closed my eyes because I knew, because before they'd shut I had seen her—arms folded down against her lower stomach, hair blown out, the arc of her stare traveling down to what I knew was on the rocks below at the margin of the ocean: flabby Abe, all tensions relaxed like a baby asleep, his blood on the stones, born to peace.

She held her lower stomach and teetered: I saw her, for my eyes would not stay closed. And I had known the voyage was coming to this. She rocked above where his body surely lay. She clutched at herself and decided.

I said "Annie? Babe?"

But she was making up her mind.

"Hey babe?"

Our father and our mother and the march back over the gravesite he had dug, the long ride in their limping car for help. The long ride back in darkness, the lights of their Ford very small. And then the walk behind the house and over the tombstones, then the wait. The motorboat throbbing from the ocean, the red lights swinging from the village to their house. Footsteps and sea swells, our mother on her hands and knees, vomiting. Our father fingering his stump. The words among men in the boat departing, the foam of their wake, the foam disappearing, Abe forever gone from Washington, the President, the church at the end of Maine. The words among the police and our parents, then everyone crushing through the pine forest and onto the tombstones. Everyone going away. Our parents staying. Our mother at the food chest in the damp kitchen: "All the ice is gone, Phil. Wouldn't you know? Tonight? That's all we need. And it must have gone before tonight. Jesus, it stinks. Why didn't I think of it? Why didn't *you?* To

180

let it go like that. It's all we need, isn't it? Jesus. God, it fucking *stinks!*"

Our father on their front steps outside, looking across the empty dark road at meadow and trees frozen by windlessness. Dropping his bone-handled sailor's knife from his forefinger, the knife dropping blade first to stand in the square he has scratched on the earth. Our father drawing a line by holding the knife as if it were a pen in his thumbless hand. Then dropping the knife from his elbow and, when the blade sticks in, drawing a line from the first one, cutting his half-a-square in half. Dropping the knife from his shoulder, the blade sticking in, the knife pulled like a pen to cut the half square in half. He scratches no initials in the boxes. He drops the knife and draws the lines, his four-fingered hand making smaller and smaller divisions. From his nose, the head arched back. From his chin. From his forehead. Now he pulls the knife like a pen through the tiniest squares. He looks across the road. The hot winds thaw the trees and then they die and everything is still. "What spoiled, babe?"

Our mother in the kitchen, sitting on the floor in front of the food chest. Her knees are crossed and she sits like a child who is watching. Her lips are open. She rubs at her head. She looks at brown butter and milk in a Mason jar that looks dark enough to be sour. Lettuce lies along a shelf like something wounded. Beer cans and wax-paper cartons are beaded with oil. The small light from the lantern she has lit is flickering, and everything in the food chest, shaped by the rhythm of the light, writhes.

Our father taps his thumb stump on the knife still stuck in the earth. "Babe? All gone?"

Our mother staring in.

Our father, tapping the knife. "Babe?"

"We'll live."

181